Tangled by Tinsel

BINDARRA CREEK CHRISTMAS ROMANCE

PHILLIPA NEFRI CLARK

Tangled by Tinsel

Cover design by Paradox
Editing by Nas Dean
Proofreading by Lia Huntington

Tangled By Tinsel

This story is set in Australia and written in Aussie/British English for an authentic experience.

Chapter One

"You have the smooshiest face ever and I just want to kiss the top of your nose over and over."

To prove her point, Miranda Layton planted a series of kisses on the bridge of Tangles's nose. Almost cross-eyed as he tried to watch her kiss him, the yellow Labrador who shared her life thumped his tail on the rug and then attempted to plant a big slurpy kiss of his own on her face.

She avoided his tongue and climbed off the floor where she'd sat to cuddle him. "Still too fast for you, my boy." Today had been long but some quality time with the love of her life was working its magic. The tension from operating beyond her normal capacity was decidedly less and a small sigh of relief left her lips. "Time for your dinner and then we'll go visit Pop before it gets too dark."

At the magic word 'dinner', Tangles wasted no time racing Miranda to the kitchen where he planted himself on the mat inside the back door. He knew not to go into the kitchen but would watch every move she made as she prepared his meal.

"So, dude. Today I managed ten clients . . . and that

isn't counting walking the hounds from up the road before I opened the salon at eight thirty." Miranda put the food bowl on the counter and went to the fridge. "I never thought I'd be able to manage ten clients in one day, but at least with Tash helping out I don't have to do the bathing now."

Tangles whined beneath his breath.

"Sorry. Here it is." She pulled out a defrosted packet of his food. Once a month she spent a few hours making and then freezing the mix of fresh meats and fish, vegetable pulp (which she made herself), and a mix of oils and vitamins. It kept him lean and as happy as a Labrador could be, considering their obsession with food.

As the dog ate, Miranda poured herself a glass of lemonade and leaned against the fridge. Her arms ached but she was proud of herself. Her grooming salon was almost fully booked until the day before Christmas Eve, and her fledgling dog walking business was taking off. Being in a position to hire a bather was something she'd never have thought possible a few months ago, but the lovely pet owners of Bindarra Creek were helping her create the business of her dreams.

Tangles licked the bowl clean and, once she'd washed it, Miranda opened the screen door and he shot outside. Being so busy meant a bit less attention for him, but he had the choice of being in the house, at the salon and shop, or visiting Pop at his leisure, so life wasn't bad for the old boy. Besides, these days he was asleep more than he was awake.

In case she was at Pop's after dark, Miranda grabbed a torch and followed Tangles as he headed up the long path to the house at the back of the property. This was the original house, where Pop and Nan lived for a decade after he retired. When Nan passed away a few years ago, Pop refused to downsize, even as his health deteriorated.

Miranda understood.

He had memories there and felt safe in the environment he loved, so it had made sense to add a small house for herself attached to her new business. Far enough away for each to have their privacy and close enough to keep an eye on him.

"That you, kiddo?" The gruff, familiar voice of her grandfather, Carter Layton, came from around the side of his house. Tangles woofed hello and disappeared along the stone path leading to the greenhouse. Nan used to grow orchids but these days Pop raised seedlings for the outdoor vegetable gardens that he and Miranda tended.

"Sure is, Pop. What are you doing out here so late?"

She hurried to take a large pot from his hands as he tried to close the greenhouse door with a foot. "Where would you like this to go?"

He reached down to pat Tangles, who leaned against his legs. "Hello, young fella."

"Pop?"

"Hm? Oh, near the front door. Thinking about putting a little tree in it for Christmas. But don't you carry it all that way."

Miranda grinned at him and kept walking. "You do know I regularly lift large dogs onto grooming tables, not to mention twenty-kilo bags of pet food, and I lug around feed for the girls." The 'girls' were two cows her grandfather insisted on keeping, more as pets than anything now that the rest of the herd he'd tended for years had passed on. They kept the grass down and he enjoyed following them around.

She placed the pot to the left of the front door. "Here, okay?"

He took a moment to climb the half dozen steps, Tangles slowly walking up them at the same time, his eyes flicking up to watch Pop. It filled Miranda's heart every time the dog picked up on her grandfather's unspoken needs and frailty. But it also broke her heart watching the once-strong man struggle with steps or lifting a pot.

"Miranda? What's wrong, child? You have a worried look on your face and now *I'm* worrying about how hard you work. Come inside." Pop led the way, followed by the dog whose tail was high and happy, and then Miranda.

Sometimes I wonder whose dog you really are.

The house was in darkness and she flicked on the hall light. Along here were a lifetime of photographs, lovingly chosen by her grandmother, then framed and hung by Pop. Several of their wedding photographs from a long-ago time when Bindarra Creek was smaller and everybody knew everyone. Then images of her parents, long deceased thanks to a dreadful accident when she was little. And plenty of her at different ages. Almost all with a dog or horse sharing the photograph. At the end were a mix of Pop's favourite shots from when he'd photographed local cricket, or landscapes. He'd always been talented with a camera.

"You eaten yet, kiddo?"

Pop's hands might shake a bit, but they still knew how to knead bread—such as the crusty loaf on the counter, and create the beautiful salad on the table, including many homegrown ingredients.

"No . . . actually, not since breakfast, which was at, hmm, well, too early." Her stomach rumbled as he took plates from a cupboard.

"Wash your hands and sit."

She wasn't about to argue. Sometimes it was nice to have him look after her the way he and Nana had done after taking her in. And she'd probably have had a frozen meal rather than take the time to make something nutritious. Hands clean, she sank onto a chair at the table. "I had ten amazing dogs to groom today, Pop. Three were brand new clients and all the owners seemed chuffed by the end results."

"Any of those fancy poodle cuts?" He sliced bread and chuckled. "Never used to see a clipped dog back in my day."

"Not today. Mostly short back and sides. That bread smells yummy. I'll get butter." She jumped up and opened the fridge, her eyes immediately drawn to a rather large slice of chocolate cake—complete with chocolate icing and cream—on a plate she didn't recognise. Her eyebrows lifted but she decided it wasn't any of her business how that delectable-looking concoction found its way to Pop's fridge. Best guess was one of the gorgeous members of CWA let him take the plate home.

"Get some of this into you. You're getting too thin." Pop added a plate of sliced bread to the table and sat. "When do you have any time for fun these days?"

Well, that's really the sixty-four thousand-dollar question.

Miranda stuffed a fork filled with tomato and cheese and onion into her mouth to give her time to think of a suitable response. Since opening the shop and salon a few months ago she'd worked harder than she imagined she could. And for longer each day that got closer to Christmas.

"Sundays. I take Sundays off." She finally announced.

He scoffed. "Apart from you cleaning that salon from top to bottom, and your house, and then working on the gardens. I mean *real* fun." Pop wiggled his eyebrows up and down. "Like a date."

She almost coughed out the bread she'd just bitten into.

"I see I hit a nerve," he said. "It is all very well, earning

5

an income and having a career, but missing love from your life is a mistake, Miranda Layton."

Seeing as he almost never used her full name, she narrowed her eyes. He winked and speared a slice of capsicum.

———

After helping wash up, Miranda said goodnight and wandered away from Pop's house with Tangles padding behind.

Pop was just being Pop. Always thinking about her wellbeing and wanting the best for his one and only grandchild.

"But you don't understand how much debt I have." She hadn't meant to speak aloud, but her tone spurred Tangle, who caught up, glancing up with a curious expression.

"We'll get through, dude. With you at my side, how could I fail?"

Back inside her little house, she made a pot of tea and opened her laptop on the kitchen table. The day's electronic takings wouldn't hit her account until tomorrow, and cash would be banked Friday in between clients—but overall, December was shaping up nicely. As long as the clients all turned up and nothing untoward happened, she'd feel comfortable about taking a break between Christmas Eve and New Year's Day.

She clicked onto her booking program. Only a half dozen appointments free between now and the last working day of the year. It wasn't hard to put a figure on the next couple of weeks—at least for grooming. There were also the dog-walking jobs and the little shop in front of the salon which was growing in popularity. If every month was like this then she could easily meet her repayments for the salon and house.

"Oh! I need to make some Christmas hampers for pets!" Miranda scribbled a note and yawned. "And sleep."

There were two lots of dogs to walk before breakfast.

No wonder she didn't have time to go on a date. Or even think about one.

Chapter Two

Kane Maxwell handed over a beer to his younger brother then dropped into the seat beside him. "Not going to say I'm not pleased to see you. But I am a bit curious why you'd leave the bright lights of Sydney behind at this time of year."

Blair had no idea how to answer so took a long mouthful of icy cold drink.

You think I lost my job.

Fair enough. Blair had arrived at Kane's home an hour ago, unannounced. Unexpected. And he had a track record of moving between jobs—at least during school and uni until he'd landed his dream position.

Last time they'd spoken was a few months ago, when Blair had to miss a family celebration because it was too far to come for the one day free he'd had. He'd felt awful about it but had a team to care for during a grand final. They kept in touch through the occasional email or text message but both were busy men with busy lives.

"Nothing like home," Blair said.

"Agree. But even so . . . no Christmas parties back there to attend? Even *I* hold a work function."

Blair shot a look at his brother and they both burst into laughter. Kane worked for himself and lived far more of a solitary life than Blair. And liked it that way.

They were sitting on the large verandah that went all the way around Kane's weatherboard house; its timber decking and railings were added by them a couple of years back. The night air was refreshing after a warm day and Blair appreciated the lower humidity of this region compared to Sydney. He was born and bred in Bindarra Creek, less than half an hour away, and on his drive home every kilometre closer to the town had made his heart a little lighter.

"Fact is that I miss you. Don't laugh at me. Mum and Dad are great, but you're my brother."

"Are you going to see them?"

"Already did," Blair said, turning the bottle in his fingers. "Stayed at Tamworth with them last night and most of the day. They're well. But . . ."

"Getting older."

Silence fell. Their parents had relocated to the bigger town when Blair moved to Sydney. They'd bought into one of the new style of retirement villages and were loving the freedom of their own home within a complex which suited their needs.

"I should have asked if I could stay here," Blair said.

Kane laughed. "Why start now?"

"No, really. What if you want to have someone over?"

"Someone?"

"A girl?"

With a shake of his head, Kane got to his feet. "There is no girl to ask. Want something to eat?" He headed inside and Blair followed, closing the front door behind himself.

His stomach growled as he helped Kane throw together some tacos.

"Still always Taco Tuesday?" he quipped. They'd had their own tradition until he moved away.

"It is Monday, mate. Have you lost time coming home?"

"Things do move slower here. So, Mex Monday it is."

"Must be some decent eateries in Sydney."

They finally sat and began to pile their plates with salad and cheese and delicious bean mix.

"I could live to one hundred and not visit every one of them. Doesn't beat this, though."

Blair hadn't realised how much tension he'd been carrying around until now. Sharing a meal with his big brother, back in his hometown, no stress, no expectations. Deep inside he sighed, letting go of the pressures of a job he enjoyed . . . well, that he didn't hate.

"Sleep well?" Kane grabbed a lunchbox and a stainless steel water bottle from the kitchen counter where he'd prepared them for the day. "I've got a group coming in so won't be back until dark. If that. Help yourself to whatever you want."

Blair headed for the kettle to make coffee. "Want me to make dinner?"

"Sure. Something reheatable though. Lock up if you leave the house." Kane was on his way out the back door.

"Since when do you . . . lock up the house?"

He was talking to the air.

Lock up in the city, for sure, but here?

Maybe being on his own made his brother paranoid, but the house—on forty acres or so—was so far off the beaten track it would take a thief with a map to find it. Nestled against the edge of the Akuna National Park, the property was one of only two on the road with a house.

And the other one, next door, hadn't been lived in for years. A long dirt road led back to Glenmeer, a small hamlet with half a dozen shops, including Kane's adventure business.

The whistle of the kettle was welcome and the coffee would kick-start his brain. He'd get an early start and drive into Bindarra Creek. Time to catch up with old friends.

"Except everyone's working," Blair muttered aloud to himself.

Instead of reuniting with mates he'd not seen in months, he was driving around town, somewhat aimlessly. People were out and about, the streets busier than he remembered, even for this time of year. Not Sydney busy, which had taken him ages to get used to. Perhaps everyone was doing their Christmas shopping early.

He already had presents for his parents and Kane. Christmas Day was a long lunch at their parents and then he and Kane would probably have a cold meal in the evening. There really wasn't anyone else to buy for. Nobody close, anyway.

Nobody special.

An odd pang of disappointment tugged at him.

It made no sense. He wasn't lonely. His work filled much of his time and he'd discovered a talent for surfing, which was what was next on his agenda after Christmas. Three weeks of surfing at some of the state's best beaches.

He realised he was driving away from town, over Kingfisher Bridge onto Bindarra Creek Road. The road curved back and forth as properties got bigger. Blair knew where he was going now and grinned. At least Miranda would be at home because she worked there. Since she'd left school she'd run a little dog-bathing business out of a shed behind her grandfather's house.

Bet things are quiet with Christmas so close.

A large A-frame sign was on the grass verge outside the property. It was brightly coloured with an arrow above the words *Dog Grooming & Shop* and a cute drawing of a dog in a bubble bath. That was new.

When he turned into the driveway he let out a long, slow whistle and came to a stop near the letterbox. Above it was a new sign. *Bindarra Creek Pampered Pets.* And about ten metres ahead, in place of the paddock he remembered, was a small, dirt carpark. But neither of those were more surprising than the building near the carpark.

A car pulled up behind him and tooted.

With a wave of his hand, he moved forward and entered the car park, choosing the spot furthest from the building. The other car parked closer and a woman climbed out, then opened the back door of her car. She lifted a small dog out and, after putting him on a lead, took him to a tree to let him relieve himself.

"Hello there, Prince!"

Miranda had emerged from the building, dressed in a smart bright purple grooming tunic, her ponytail swinging as she met the woman halfway. She squatted to greet the dog, who clearly knew her. And adored her, judging from the rapid wagging of his tail. As she straightened with Prince in her arms, she glanced across at Blair's car. She wouldn't recognise this new one and with the tinting, most likely couldn't see in. A moment later, the woman returned to her car and Miranda disappeared inside.

The building was exactly like a shop you'd see in a street in town. One wide display window and an entry with two glass doors. Across the window the name of the business was emblazoned in bright purple—the same colour as Miranda's top.

"You did it. You said you would." Blair locked the car, shaking his head as he crossed the carpark. She'd always talked about a proper grooming salon. A place to give her a full-time income and let her do what she loved every day. But how had she accomplished so much in the months he'd been away? Building this, permits, design, fitout—it was a big job.

A sudden thought struck him and he stopped near the window.

Are you married?

Just as quickly he pushed the thought away. It wouldn't matter. Miranda was resourceful, hardworking, and focused. She wouldn't need a man in her life to help with the heavy lifting. And he couldn't quite believe he'd thought that. Unless it was from some other part of him— a spot in his heart. The part which had always felt just a fraction closer to her than she did to him.

"Coming in, Blair? I have work to do and can't have a strange man skulking around my shopfront to scare off the customers."

Chapter Three

Blair Maxwell was the last person Miranda expected to see in her carpark. Wasn't he in the city looking after the torn muscles and sore feet of a fancy football team? She gently lowered Prince into a playpen. "Tash will be here soon so sit tight." Prince wagged his tail, his big eyes shining.

Outside, Blair was staring at the shop with the strangest series of expressions crossing his face. The first one had to be surprise.

Shocked I made my dream come true?

She allowed herself a short laugh. In the past few years, her best friend from school had been back and forward to Bindarra Creek while he attended university for his degree and then work experience in Armidale. His dream of working with a high-profile football club came true early in the year and she was proud of him. But she'd always had a suspicion he thought her own dream was unattainable.

"Boys. What do they know?"

The surprised look turned into something else . . . What *was* he thinking? For an instant she thought she'd seen—well, panic. Trick of the light. She pushed open the door.

"Coming in, Blair? I have work to do and can't have a strange man skulking around my shopfront to scare off the customers."

He grinned and the minute he was inside, she threw her arms around his neck. And just as fast, she dropped them and stepped back. She was certain her face had reddened.

"Um . . . okay, well hello to you too." Blair smiled broadly and she went from embarrassment to a peculiar urge to smack his arm.

Folding her own arms, she looked him up and down. "No tatts?"

"Huh? No."

"Just figured being a footie person you'd be covered by now."

"I'm a sports physio, not a player. Getting tatts isn't on my bucket list." He gazed around the interior. "This is impressive, Miranda."

"A whole lot of work and love went into it. *And* money." That last bit was enough to extinguish any warmth. Too much money. "I have to keep going so feel free to follow me around."

"Just like the old days."

She shot him a look. His sparkling eyes told her he was teasing. There had been a time during the early high school years when Blair did follow her around . . . not in a creepy way of course. But his brother had finished school and Blair was a loner thanks to a couple of bullies. Miranda was a bit the same and they'd made friends after being in the school play.

The friendship continued over the years and it was only when their friends, other loners they'd collected into their circle, tried to pair them up romantically that they both took a step back. He'd been leaving for uni anyway, so it wasn't as if they'd just stopped talking.

I'd never want to lose you.

Well, that was an odd thought!

"Good morning!"

Thank goodness for Tash.

Fresh out of high school, Tash was a cheery and hard-working lass who loved their clients even more than Miranda, if that was possible. With red hair in a plait, freckles, and a perpetual smile, Tash spent her days washing and drying dogs, clipping nails, and looking after the shop in turns with Miranda.

"Morning, Tash. King is waiting for you."

"Yay! The usual?" Tash was on her way to his pen and the little dog whined in delight as she approached. "Hello, little man."

"Sure thing. Pancho was dropped off early so I've bathed him and will clip him next." Starting the day ahead of schedule might buy her a bit of time at the end of the day. She'd not had a chance to decorate yet and was longing to add some Christmas joy to the shop.

Remembering Blair was there, she spun back. "I am sorry but I really need to get to work."

"Can I help?"

"Can you clip a dog? Like, properly?"

He tilted his head to the left then right and back again with a silly look on his face. "I'll try."

"No trying. They are not sheep. Or alpacas. My clients expect their beloved pets to be *professionally* groomed. Anything else you can offer?"

"Massage?"

Miranda circled her shoulders without realising and when she did, she laughed. "Sounds wonderful. After a full day grooming I ache in places I didn't know existed."

His eyebrows raised.

That silly blush returned and she quickly went behind the counter and collected a file. "How long are you home?"

"Till after Christmas. Staying with Kane. Anyway, go work." At the door he turned. "I'd love to catch up and hear all about this. When you have time."

"Oh. Okay. Yes, that sounds good. I'm usually finished by six each night if you want to drop by? Come and see Pop." Now she was waffling on. Whatever was wrong with her?

"Good stuff. I'll see you later."

Later, when? Today? Next week? A year?

But he just winked and then left, sauntering across the carpark to what looked like a new SUV. He'd done well for himself. Carved out the life he wanted.

Good for you, Blair. I'm proud.

Home for Christmas? Then back to his new life.

Miranda pushed down sudden sadness. She didn't know where it came from and, quite frankly, didn't have time or the bandwidth to deal with it.

"I can fit Bruno in, Mrs. Marron. If he just needs a bath and tidy, then there is a spot tomorrow at two." Miranda was on the phone, pen in hand as she wrote notes. "Just confirming that Bruno is a maltese cross who is regularly clipped and just needs his face, feet, and sanitary areas tidied? And he has a calm nature, you said? Uh huh. I have one hour free and he'll be ready for you to collect at three. Bring him in at ten to two. Okay, see you then."

With new dogs Miranda tried to get extra information as owners didn't always know how their dog behaved when away from home. She didn't accept known biters because a dog bite could put her or Tash out of action for days.

There were a few dogs she groomed who were nervous and she always ensured they had longer than usual appointments so that they had time to settle. At least now with Tash here every day, she had a reliable and calm assistant if she needed an extra set of hands with a client.

The shop itself was the busiest Miranda remembered and the small gain of time she'd made earlier in the day disappeared with serving customers. So many people commented on the retail area and asked for gift ideas. Not having any idea how she'd find the time, Miranda promised to have some Christmas hampers and goodies ready by Saturday, being the second to last weekend before Christmas.

"Decorate the shop. Create hampers. Groom dogs. Walk dogs. And so on," she said to the air as she locked the front door. "You've got this, Miranda."

Tash had cleaned up after the last dog left and was on her way to a Christmas party. By the time Miranda turned off the lights and checked one more time that everything was where it should be, it was a bit after six. She peered into the carpark. No shiny new SUV.

Exactly what did you expect? He has other people to see.

Tangles wasn't at home so Miranda walked up to Pop's house to collect him. He was such a good dog. Never strayed off the property and tended to keep to his bed behind the counter if he was in the shop. Much as he loved a pat, he seemed to understand it was a workplace and would only wander out to greet someone he knew. Mind you, that meant a lot of people.

He was waiting at the front door as she climbed the steps.

"How come the lights are all off?"

Bit pointless asking the dog but it was unusual to find the place so quiet. Pop always put the outside lights on for her even though it was still light at this hour. Maybe he'd fallen asleep reading.

"Shall we find Pop?" Miranda let them both into the house and Tangles trotted toward the kitchen as she called. "Just us, Pop. Whereabouts are you?"

She checked the rooms as she went. Not in the living room, or dining room, or his study, which was really his reading area. Nor his bedroom. And finding the kitchen empty of her grandfather and with the lights off sent alarm bells off.

He'd wandered off a couple of times recently. On both occasions he'd said he was just having a walk but had seemed a bit lost. Was he really losing his bearings? What if she couldn't find him this time?

What if she lost him . . . she couldn't lose anyone else. She just couldn't.

Chapter Four

Pull yourself together. Panic fixes nothing.

Pop might be ageing but he had a clean bill of health, including his mental capacity. If there was one thing that Nan's passing had done, it was to galvanise Pop into regular health checks. She'd left it too late after finding the lump in her breast. Her dying words were for him to do better for himself, and he had.

So where might he be? Miranda hadn't noticed him drive out earlier—he'd have to pass the shop—but then again, her focus was on the dogs and customers. Even so, it wasn't his usual shopping day and there were no appointments marked on the calendar on the fridge. And it was later than he'd normally be out.

Miranda, followed closely by Tangles, went through the back door.

"Pop? Pop, where are you?" Her voice sounded strained to her ears. He wasn't in the greenhouse. The only other place might be at the big shed where he kept the feed and stuff for the cows. But that was a waste of time and she ran back to the house. She'd try his mobile number and if that didn't find him, she'd call the police.

There really wasn't anyone else she could think of to help. Blair's face weirdly popped into her mind and she pushed it away.

Almost back at the house, Tangles hurtled off around the side and barked his welcome woof.

Heart racing, Miranda followed the sound.

Pop's car approached up the driveway.

Why didn't I check the garage?

Before his car reached her she had the tilt door open and he drove straight in, popping the boot before climbing out.

"Well, this is service!"

"Where were you?"

He gave her a smile. "Shopping, of course. For Christmas." The boot had several bags of shopping—not from Bindarra Creek by the look of the retailers' logos.

She grabbed as many as she could manage but one was really heavy and he insisted on taking it, pulling down the door as they left.

I want to hug you and yell at you!

Her full arms prevented the first urge and her manners stopped the second. The time it took to reach the kitchen was sufficient to calm down enough to avoid saying something she'd regret. Something said out of fear.

"I've got a bit of grocery shopping as well, so can you empty these bags for me and I'll go and hide the rest." He winked and took all but two bags from her.

Although both of them preferred to shop in Bindarra Creek, every so often they'd go further afield where there were different options. Pop had clearly been to one of the bigger supermarkets in the next big town and had stocked up on his favourite tinned tuna and a brand of biscuits he liked. There was also a bottle of brandy. What on earth was this for? Neither of them drank it. She was holding it when he returned.

"Christmas cake, kiddo. I think there is just enough time to make one if I prepare the fruit tomorrow."

Tears prickled at the back of her eyes and she lowered the bottle onto the kitchen counter, not wanting Pop to see her upset. Nan always made Christmas cake. Every year for as long as Miranda could remember. Pop didn't make cakes. And since Nan had died . . .

Pop's arms went around her and, with a sob, Miranda turned and leaned her head on his shoulder. He patted her back for a few minutes until she regained control. "Sorry," she mumbled.

"Go get a tissue. And never be sorry for missing your nan. I do, every single day."

She helped herself to a few tissues, blowing her nose and dabbing her eyes while Pop poured them both glasses of water.

"Nan made the best Christmas cake and I'm not aiming to reach those exacting standards, but she wrote the recipe down and it will be made with love, just like she'd have wanted." There was a suspicious glisten in his own eyes. "You were worried about where I was?"

Eyes mostly dry, Miranda nodded. "I should have checked the garage first. Tangles was up here and waiting outside which seemed unusual, so I let myself in. And checked the greenhouse. And the girls' paddock." She forced a laugh. "I was about to send up smoke signals."

Pop headed for the fridge and extracted a bottle of white wine. He poured a glass for Miranda and then himself. "You got a scare. I drove past when you had a busy carpark and didn't think to leave a note. The plan was to be home an hour ago but . . ." Just before he took a sip, a curious little smile touched his lips.

Whatever are you up to?

Well, Pop was old enough to manage his own life.

Maybe he'd caught up with some friends. The wine tasted good and on her empty stomach it gave her a warm glow.

"Staying for dinner?"

"Can't tonight. Customers are asking for some Christ-massy gifts so I want to spend a bit of time planning what can be made into hampers or little gift packs. At least then Tash and I can make them up between clients."

"Can I help?"

"Oh, you don't have to do that." Then she grinned. "Maybe. Let me work it all out and if I get stuck, I'll let you know."

Perhaps Pop wouldn't mind wrapping some hampers. She didn't want to impose but she'd also never experienced Christmas as a business owner and was astonished by how many new customers she was getting.

"Guess who dropped by the shop today?"

Over his glass, Pop gave her one of those looks . . . an 'it could be anyone' kind of look.

"Blair."

Now, his eyebrows shot up. "Blair Maxwell?"

"The very one."

"Tired of Sydney already? Do you know, I lived in the city for a few months in my early twenties—about the same age Blair is now. Quite the experience."

"Yes. You *have* told me this before. And then you saw the error of your ways and came back to Bindarra Creek to propose marriage to Nan."

He laughed.

"Anyway, Blair is on a break and visiting Kane for the holidays. Guess he'll see his parents as well while he's here."

"Guess?"

"He dropped in when I had dogs to clip. Wasn't an awful lot of time to chat but he said he's staying until after

Christmas. And he has a fancy new SUV so life must be treating him well."

"Ah."

"Ah?"

"Miss having him drop by. Talking cricket and footie. Nice young man with a good attitude and talent. My knee never worked as well as after he practiced on it a couple of years back. Hm. Wonder if he'd take another look?" Pop finished his wine.

"Well, if he comes back I'll ask him."

"Oh, Miranda. Of course he'll be back and probably to stay eventually. Your Nan used to say that Blair was perfect for you, and you for him."

Heat rushed up from her neck to the scalp. This wasn't helpful. She quickly drained her glass and washed it. "I'd better get going and feed Tangles."

The dog's head shot up. He'd been asleep near the door.

"Thanks for checking up on me and I am sorry for the scare. I'll try to leave a note if I head out."

She leaned up to kiss his cheek. "Thank you. And I shall try to do the same, although I don't really go anywhere." On her way to the door, she glanced back. "After Christmas I have a short break planned. I'll spend more time with you."

"My dear Miranda. You are here so often checking up on me. Taking care of me. And I love that you do, but I'd like to see you spend time with a young man."

"Ha. Not for years. I'm way too busy to worry about romance."

"Life is too short to miss out on love." Pop nodded. "Don't rule it out."

Chapter Five

Two days home and Blair was bored. Perhaps not bored, as that wasn't in his nature but with everyone he knew being so busy he felt a bit . . . well, on the outside.

Kane was a leave-early, return-late kind of person thanks to his adventure tours in the national park, so they'd seen each other only in passing since the first night. Of his old male friends, only two still lived in town and both were now raising young families. There'd been invitations to dinner on the weekend, but until then he was at a loose end. And his standby person who'd always been up for a walk or a coffee was up to her neck in grooming dogs.

He sat outside at the Cypress Café, people-watching while he sipped a milkshake through a brightly coloured paper straw. There was nothing like a Bindarra Creek chocolate-malt milkshake and if there'd been any apple turnovers left, he'd have devoured one of those. It was too long after lunch to expect those tasty treats to not be sold out.

Miranda's grandmother had baked nice stuff—mini pies and cakes for afternoon tea—more than once when he visited. He sighed and finished the milkshake. Nanna

Layton was what he and his friends called her. Sadly passed away now. He'd been up to the house a couple of times since then and given Pop Layton a hand moving the cows or mowing the large expanse of lawn in the home paddock. His labour seemed like a fair swap for the years of delicious food.

Blair wandered away from the café as it neared its closing time, enjoying stretching his legs without the push and shove of Sydney. The shops were looking festive with their decorations and although the window displays were nothing as grand as those of the themed city department stores, somehow they were more . . . real.

Kane hadn't bothered decorating his house. Probably no point when he lived on his own and was out every daylight hour. But Blair liked Christmas, with the sparkle and music and food and presents.

And the people.

A young couple walked toward him, their fingers entwined and their spare hands carrying bags. Red tinsel peeped out of one, glinting in the afternoon sun.

Christmas needs to be spent with people you care about.

The thought was accompanied by a deep restlessness. He had everything he needed in his life though. Didn't he?

Half an hour later, he piled several bags of his own into the car. He'd surprise Kane with decorations. And dinner. But as soon as he got behind the wheel there was a beep from his phone with a message from his brother.

Staying overnight up at the guest house near the river. Sorry about dinner. And we need to talk about Christmas Day.

Kane was away tonight then. The upside was having the house to himself for the night so he could decorate as much as he wanted and grab something unhealthy to heat up later.

The downside . . .

Blair gazed at himself in the rear-vision mirror. Why

did he look so lost? This wasn't typical of a man who'd spent the last few years challenging himself and exceeding his own expectations. Nor of a man who'd left everything he knew and loved in order to pursue a career he'd strived for. Resilience was his middle name.

Sometimes resilience needed company.

With a grin he climbed back out of the car and located some shopping bags. He knew someone else who loved making things pretty. And she had to eat sometime or other.

Chapter Six

Miranda sorted tinsel, separating the strands which had gotten themselves tangled in the shopping bags. Tash had run out earlier and bought thick red and gold tinsel, baubles, and a small artificial tree which was ready to set up in the window complete with a star on top.

Her day had not gone to plan—far from it—at least after lunch, which she had missed.

Bruno—who, according to his owner, was a calm and friendly dog who enjoyed his grooms and only needed a tidy up—was, in fact, the devil incarnate.

She should have turned him away when he arrived. The dog clearly hadn't been groomed in months, with a thick, matted coat and a 'get away from me' expression. But her heart couldn't let him deal with the heat in such poor condition and she'd told his owner she'd phone when he was ready and to expect the cost to be higher than quoted, given his state.

The dog might have been small, but he made up for it with a ferocity and attitude more fitting a much larger creature.

Like a jackal. Or gargoyle.

Tash had distracted him with treats during his first clip, which wasn't too bad, but then he'd tried to bite her when she bathed him. Miranda heard her squeal as she pulled her hand away just in time, and left a customer to check on her.

"You take over in the shop for me and I'll manage Mr. Cranky Pants, okay?" She'd insisted Tash leave him with her. Fast reflexes had saved her from bites more than once and they got a workout with Bruno. He was even worse with the dryer, grabbing the nozzle several times. There was no way she could do the final clip without Tash's help and between them they lost almost an hour of precious time by going so slowly with him. It wasn't the best job she'd ever done, but the matting was gone and he actually wagged his tail at them both as if feeling better.

Mrs. Marron returned for him in a mood. She didn't appreciate Bruno taking so long. And while she admitted he looked much better, the colour had risen in her face at the register.

"That is almost twice what you quoted! I wouldn't pay so much for my own hair."

Holding back an urge to mention hairdressers didn't generally deal with biting and coat neglect, Miranda put the sale through and said a cheery goodbye.

Thank goodness the rest of the clients for the day were regulars and she and Tash powered through to finish close to the normal time. She'd sent Tash home and cleaned up. Pop had Tangles for the night so she grabbed a ladder and made a start on the decorations.

She turned most of the lights off to save power, using the natural early evening light. The ladder allowed her to just reach the ceiling which was made up of moveable panels. It was easy to twist a tinsel tie around one end of a strand and then hook it beneath a panel. Gracious curves of sparkling colour fanning out like a flower from the middle of the shop was what she'd had in mind.

Up the ladder. Hook the tinsel in. Climb down. Move the ladder. Repeat.

This ladder is getting taller every time I climb it.

Exhaustion from the day was setting in and she was starving. A sensible person would go and eat but she didn't expect decorating to take more than a couple of hours to finish.

At the top of the ladder Miranda lost control of the tinsel whose other end was already secured a few metres away. She grabbed and missed; it came to a rest on top of one of her product stands.

"Come here." Arm outstretched, she reached, but it was a little too far.

Perhaps if she went up a rung . . . This time her finger-tips brushed the tinsel. Tantalisingly close. A little bit more and she'd have it.

The ladder lifted a fraction.

She adjusted her stance and reached again.

Touch the tinsel. Yes. Almost . . .

A shriek filled her ears as the ladder tilted.

Air was all around her.

Pain sliced through her leg as she hit the ground.

The ladder crashed into the concrete.

Somebody was moaning nearby.

The tiled floor was cold and hard against her shoulder and hip.

With a slight movement, it all rushed back and Miranda's eyes shot open. She'd fallen.

Lay still. Breathe.

She was numb.

The pain in her leg was gone.

But there was a weird tapping coming from somewhere.

Tap.

Tap, tap, tap.

"Miranda! How do I get in?"

What is Blair doing here?

Lifting her head a bit, she spotted him at the front door. It was locked, of course. Why would he think it was open? Oh, where was he going? She let her head sink back onto the floor but kept her eyes open. Beneath the closest product stand, a pair of shoes appeared. How odd. She was sure there weren't any shoes in the shop.

"Stay still."

"Did you break in?" Why did her voice sound so weird?

The shoes disappeared. Blair's face came into view, really close.

"Hello," she said.

His eyes were the warmest shade of brown. There were tiny flecks of gold in them. How come she'd never noticed?

"Do you know if you hit your head?"

Her mind was less fuzzy. She wanted to get up.

"No."

"No you didn't hit your head or no you don't remember?"

"I didn't hit my head."

"Are you sure, Miranda? I tapped for ages before you responded."

"I was kinda shocked. I closed my eyes on the way down but I landed on my feet . . . I think." The numbness was receding. "And my ankle buckled and I ended up face planting."

"Okay, we'll sit you up slowly, but if you feel dizzy or anything, just say."

"We? How many people are with you?"

There was no answer but the warm hands gently guiding her into a sitting position did all kinds of weird things to her. He kept them there, one behind her back and the other holding one of her hands and all the time, those eyes of his never left hers.

"Still okay?" He shuffled into a kneeling position.

"Think so. Can't believe I fell off the ladder. Can you see if I broke it?"

"Later. I want to be certain you didn't break."

She giggled. She never giggled. Her heart was pounding. And her ankle hurt. A lot. Miranda tentatively moved it and gasped. "Ow . . . oh no."

"Ankle?"

All she could do was nod.

Those gentle hands moved to the offending part of her leg and she held her breath as he moved it a little, this way then that. "Doubt there's a break but you need to see a doctor. Actually, best to have an X-ray to be sure. I'll take you."

Hospital? Now?

She shook her head. "I have to finish the decorations, Blair. If you don't mind helping me bandage it then I'll—"

"You'll what, Miranda?" He leaned back on his heels. "Climb up and down the ladder some more? Decorations will be the least of your worries if there is a fracture. You need some anti-inflammatories and proper strapping on the ankle at the very least and although I can do the latter, I don't carry drugs around just in case somebody decides to cut corners with their health."

Fine. It wouldn't take long and she'd be able to finish this when she got back.

"We might need to let Pop know. He'll worry if he comes to visit."

"Phone him on the way. I'm going to bring the car

closer. Can I go through the front door? I'll grab your handbag and keys and stuff and lock the back door."

Blair didn't wait for an answer and Miranda found herself alone again.

Her ankle throbbed. Her back hurt. And all she wanted was to curl up in a ball and cry, but she didn't have time for that. She didn't have time to stop.

Chapter Seven

The drive back from the hospital was quiet. Blair glanced at Miranda periodically, a hot mess of feelings still churning as they'd been since he'd seen her fall. He'd told himself to shelve the emotion overload until later. For now, Miranda needed someone to be calm and strong for her.

But those seconds kept playing in his mind.

He'd parked in the carpark after seeing movement in the shop. Miranda was working late, up a ladder, making the shop pretty for Christmas and from outside, it looked a picture already. Hand raised to knock, he'd stopped as she leaned to reach for something, not wanting to distract her. Had he made the right decision? Because seconds later, the ladder tipped and she toppled off.

His heart had leapt into his throat as, arms and legs flailing, she'd disappeared behind a stand, only her face in his line of sight, and that was covered by her hair. He'd started tapping the door, willing her to jump to her feet with that cheeky grin and wave at him. The minutes had passed and he was about to find something to break the glass when she moved.

It finally occurred to him to run around to the back of

the shop. Except there was a small house attached, and its back door was unlocked. By the time he'd navigated his way through her house, finding a connecting door and then finally reaching the shop, she was more coherent.

"Blair?"

He realised he'd come to a stop on the turn-off to Bindarra Creek Road. It was pitch black outside and there was no other traffic in sight.

"Hey. You doing okay?" He turned onto the road.

"What will I do?"

Her voice was so low he had to strain to hear her words.

"It isn't a broken bone. That is fantastic news, Miranda. Okay?"

"I guess."

"The sprain will heal and I can help with some exercises to strengthen the ankle in a few days. If you'd like." He snuck a look at her face, which was pale and serious and worried. "And the anti-inflams will ease the pain as well as reduce the swelling."

"Why were you there? At the shop?"

It seemed silly now.

"Are we going to your Pop's house?"

"No. Mine, thanks. Pop's keeping Tangles for the night and I let him know what's been happening."

A minute later he'd parked beside Miranda's car, behind her house. In an instant he was out and around to open the passenger door.

"I can open a door, Blair."

"Yes, but can you—"

"What? Walk? No but I'll hobble." She climbed out and touched her injured foot to the ground with a soft, 'ouch.'

"Which wasn't what I was about to say. Can you find the keys to the door so I can put some lights on first?"

"Oh."

While she dug around in her handbag, leaning back against the car, he took a carry bag out of the back seat.

She held out the keys. "This one opens the door. The back light is just inside . . . What's in the bag?"

"Can you stay here for a minute and I'll be right back."

He wasn't waiting for an answer. He left the head-lights on, which helped him make it to the door without incident, dodging a drying rack full of towels and three dog beds made of metal frames with legs and canvas covers. If he tripped and ended up face down on the grass with a sprain, they'd both be hobbling around. Once the light was on, he dropped the bag inside and sprinted back.

He offered his arm.

She shook her head. "I can manage."

"Or I could carry you. Why are you being so stubborn?"

"You wouldn't."

"Your choice."

The look she cast him was familiar. Miranda had never let anyone do things for her. She was great in a team and always, always helped other people without being asked, but when it came to her own needs she put up barriers.

She took his arm with a subdued huff which made him want to laugh aloud. He didn't.

"Would you like me to bring the towels in soon? And the beds?"

"I can manage."

"Did you just say that through gritted teeth? No, you will follow the doctor's orders and sit somewhere comfort-able with your ankle up and let me help out, just for tonight."

Oddly, instead of the argument he expected, her grip tightened. When he glanced at her face, there were tears in

36

her eyes. Before she could say a word he scooped her up in his arms. "Slow-poke. I bet you've not eaten tonight."

She leaned her head against his shoulder and something stirred in his heart. If only she'd let him help out without a fight. If only she hadn't fallen.

What is wrong with you, Maxwell?

He pushed the feeling away and got them both through the door. "Where's the living room?"

"Straight ahead."

Blair stopped just inside a doorway to let Miranda find the light switch. The room was small but cosy with comfortable furniture and muted colours. He lowered her onto the sofa then grabbed a couple of cushions and gently adjusted her injured foot. "Is this okay?"

"Stop fussing. I'm fine. All I need are those tablets and I'll get some water and have them and . . ."

Eyes huge, Miranda bit her lip as she gazed at him.

He squatted beside her. "Tell you what. You sit tight for a few minutes and first I'll get some ice for the ankle and then I'll feed us both. See, I had this idea earlier . . . long story. Those tablets are best taken with food, okay. And I happen to have come prepared."

"For this?" She gestured at her ankle, strapped at the hospital but obviously swollen. "I have two families expecting me to walk their dogs at seven in the morning." She shuffled herself so she was more upright. "Then a full day of grooming. I haven't finished decorating. I need to make hampers. Pop said he'll help but I have to put them together first. And that is just tomorrow. What about the next day? And the next?"

Her lips quivered and there was a suspicious glean in her eyes.

"What if you call the families to explain?" He glanced at his watch. "A bit late now, but first thing in the morning."

"They've both pre-paid walks right up until Christmas Eve because they are so busy themselves. I can't let seven dogs miss their walks because of . . . this."

Seven? In two families? How do you walk them?

Miranda swung her foot off the cushions and sat right up. "Seriously, I have no choice, Blair. The salon and shop only opened a few months ago and the money is coming in faster than I dreamed. But it's money I need to pay the bills. Pay for the buildings. And I cannot . . . no, I *will not* let my clients down. I just can't."

With that, she burst into tears.

"Don't cry. Oh, Miranda . . . it'll be alright. Really."

She couldn't have heard him as her face was in her hands and her shoulders shook. Blair put his arms around her and she melted against him and sobbed. He patted her back and made soothing sounds but had no idea how to fix this.

I'll think of something. Hang in there, Miranda.

Chapter Eight

Blair helped her limp to the bathroom where she washed her face and took a few minutes to rein in the panic. Her eyes were huge as she stared at herself, and her skin was so pale. She redid her ponytail and rubbed her cheeks.

"I'll fix this," she whispered to her reflection. "I'm tough."

Almost the instant she opened the door, Blair appeared from the kitchen.

Oh goodness, I wept all over the poor man.

She avoided his eyes by looking at his chest—which was a mistake because his t-shirt was damp where her face had been. He'd been so kind. Comforting. And he smelt nice.

Her eyes shot up to his, even as her face heated up. The corners of his lips were flickering up and down, as though he was trying to control the need to laugh. She lifted her chin. "Thank you for helping me, Blair. For taking me to the hospital and . . . well, everything. I'll be fine to manage now."

"I piled the beds on top of each other under your

porch and carried the towel rack inside. Do they need to be folded and go into the salon?"

"Not tonight they don't."

Clearly he wasn't getting the hint.

"And I checked that the ladder is fine and no products were damaged. You are the only casualty." Blair crossed his arms and gazed at her.

This wasn't the boy who'd been her best mate at school. Not even the young man working his backside off to excel at his studies. Was a year away from Bindarra Creek what had changed Blair? Made him all . . . grown up? Bossy?

"Before you turf me through the door, hear me out. Please, Miranda."

Standing up this long was beginning to hurt. A lot. She shifted most of her weight onto her good leg.

He noticed and took her arm. "You never answered me earlier about when you last ate."

She found herself being quite firmly directed back to the living room and finally gave up when the sofa appeared. She needed to sit.

"Maybe lunchtime? Might have been breakfast. For the tablets?" The sofa felt good.

Blair adjusted her leg again and this time, rested the ankle on an ice pack wrapped in a tea towel. How long had she been in the bathroom? He had covered a lot of ground.

More than I can.

She gulped down the rising tide of tears. No more.

"Do you still like cheese?" he asked.

"Love cheese. But . . ."

He'd turned and was heading out of the room.

"Be right back."

Years ago on a school excursion to Scone, they'd gone to a cheese factory. As stinky as it was there, Miranda and

Blair had been the two teens who'd tried every style of cheese laid out in samples. While other kids had made off with the hard cheeses, they'd compared notes about locally made blue and soft ones. How funny to remember such a thing.

Her stomach growled and she put both hands on it to cover the sound. Pop was always on at her to eat properly and maybe it was time to start listening. If she'd eaten rather than climbing up and down the ladder, she might have made better judgements. And not be in this mess. "But you are."

"Now, I brought wine but that doesn't go well with anti-inflammatories so it's in your fridge for another time." Blair carried a tray in. Had he been through all her kitchen cupboards, because she didn't remember where the wooden tray was kept. He placed it on the coffee table. There were two plates, both piled high with what seemed a ton of food. Several types of cheese with relish, different crackers, olives, pickles, and some kind of dip.

"But . . . why?"

He put one plate on the coffee table and, after she'd shuffled to move more onto her side with the bad leg still supported, he settled the tray on the sofa. There was a fork and napkin and a glass of water. Plus the tablets.

"Why the food? Hm. I was in town earlier and saw people shopping for decorations." He took his plate and sat on the armchair. "Kane has done nothing to get his house ready for Christmas so I bought tinsel and baubles and stuff. Best to take the tablets before you eat." He bit into a piece of cheese.

The aroma of cheese and relish had Miranda's stomach begging for food but she pushed two tablets onto her palm and swallowed them with some water.

"So I went back to his house and spent a couple of hours dressing it up. He's doing some overnight trips with

41

clients so I knew I'd be eating alone, and thought if you were as well then maybe we could eat together. And catch up. You were so busy yesterday."

"I often eat with Pop." Miranda scooped some dip onto a cracker and crunched into it.

"Except you didn't tonight."

"Huh? How do you know?" Next into her mouth was a piece of tasty cheese with relish on top and it was delicious.

"Actually, I called here and spoke to Tash. She said you were planning on starting the decorations straight after work. Even if you'd eaten, I figured a cheesy picnic would come in handy after we'd finished."

"Finished?"

"I enjoy decorating. Always up for hanging tinsel."

Miranda knew she was at the point of exhaustion and wasn't in a good state of mind, thanks to recent events, but even so, why didn't it make sense?

He likes decorating so brought me dinner? And wine?

She stopped chewing and looked at Blair. Really looked at him. He was intent on piling one of everything onto a round biscuit. He had a three-day growth which suited his face. His jeans and t-shirt, which followed the contours of his body, testified that he was fit. Fitter than she'd ever seen. Or noticed, anyway.

Was this meant to be a date?

Her mouthful stuck in her throat and she grabbed the glass of water as a tide of panic whooshed up. Different from her earlier anxious response, this was about feelings. And she didn't want to explore hers. Not now. Maybe not ever. They were friends and it needed to stay that way because . . . she didn't have time.

"Why do you look so suspicious?" Blair asked.

"I don't know what you mean."

He tilted his head, eyes narrowing. "Have I done something wrong?"

How on earth could she explain that he'd done everything right? Helped her after the fall. Taken her to and from the hospital. Made her as comfortable as she could be. And fed her.

Yeah. And now you want to date me.

Forcing a smile she shook her head. "Nothing at all. I'm terribly tired and have an early start . . ."

"Well, eat as much as you want and then I'll clean up and get out of your hair. Unless you'd rather I sleep here tonight? I mean, on the sofa, but that way I'm close by if—"

"No! Um, I mean, no I couldn't do that to you."

"It would mean I'm already here rather than driving back early in the morning."

"Back?"

"You *are* tired. Those dogs to walk in the morning? I'm pretty handy with my legs and you know I love animals."

The piece of cheese she'd just picked up fell from her fingers. "Blair, you can't do that!"

"Then tell me what your plan is."

Seven dogs to walk between seven and eight in the morning. She'd have breakfast at six and swallow more tablets. And pain killers if need be. A pair of decent walking boots and she'd be fine. A bit sore, but fine. Then her eyes moved to her ankle, aloft on the pillows. And swollen. There was no chance she'd get a boot onto it.

"Miranda? I'm bored silly. I came home without anyone knowing I was heading back and as a result all of my friends, and my own brother, are committed to the eyeballs, with Christmas being so close. Take the other day when I dropped in and you already had groomed one dog and had another one waiting."

"I'm sorry."

His smile disarmed her.

"Don't be. I can't believe what you've done for yourself

this year and all I wanted was to come and enjoy a glass of wine with my best friend and hear all about it."

I'm still just your best friend? Oh, thank goodness.

"But why are you bored? Did living in Sydney stop you enjoying solitude?"

The strangest expression flickered across his face, gone as quickly as it came.

He shrugged. "The point is, I guess, that I'd love to be useful. So, let me take over the doggy walks until the ankle is better. Will you be okay to sit and groom dogs?"

Tash could manage the shop and wash dogs . . . as long as the shop wasn't too busy. And she could perch on a stool to groom.

"I can. Are you certain? I'm unsure how long before I can properly walk and—"

"I'm sure. Look, it is only for the rest of this week and next. Then you have a break. Which means no grooming, or shop, or dogs to walk, right?"

She nodded.

"Then it's settled," he said.

"I'll pay you, Blair."

"No chance."

"This only happens if I pay you."

For a long moment they stared at each other. And just when she was convinced he'd changed his mind, he nodded. "If that's what it takes. I'll be here bright and early for my first assignment."

Chapter Nine

"Slow down, Scrappy . . . Scruffy? Anyway, whoever is pulling like mad, please stop. You have me for half an hour and it isn't a race."

Two leads in each hand, Blair increased his pace to keep up with his charges who knew the route better than he remembered from the map Miranda handed him earlier. She'd had everything organised. A walking belt complete with poop bags and a spare collar, portable water bowl and a full bottle to clip onto his belt. And a brief on each dog with their name, description, personality, and anything to watch for.

"Like trying to trick their new walker," he muttered.

Miranda's route for this second group included cutting across the showground and a stop at the river. It was designed as a decent work out and it was. By the time Blair returned the four happy pooches to their owner, they were showing signs of slowing down and so was he.

He stopped to collect takeaway coffees on the way back to Miranda's. She'd been much more her usual self when he tapped on the door at six-thirty but he'd seen her wince as she moved from the door to the kitchen table where she'd prepared his walking kit. Not wasting any time, she'd run him through the routine, told him the first address, then sent him off.

The front door of the salon was open when he parked in the carpark. The shop didn't open until nine but Miranda accepted the first couple of dogs in for grooming earlier. Her hours must be huge each week.

Joys of owning a small business.

Miranda was on a stool behind the counter, head in her hands. A lined notebook was open in front of her.

Unwilling for her to think he'd seen her like that, Blair stepped outside again, took a moment, then began to cheerily whistle as he walked back in. Her head shot up and she pushed the book aside, her face moving from despair to welcome in an instant.

"Coffee?"

"You legend." Her eyes lit up. "I've yet to have one. And before you say anything, I did have some toast after you left so I could take the medication. How was it? You obviously survived."

"No thanks to Ruby the Rottweiler who took a liking to a duck in the river and almost dragged me in."

She laughed. "Whoops, I forgot to add how much she loves taking a dip. Apart from that was everything alright though?"

He sipped his coffee, leaning his hip against the counter. "All the dogs were lovely. Really cool and easy to walk . . . well, apart from Scruffy who thinks he leads the pack—including me."

"Well, you are new to him. No doubt he viewed you as bottom of the heap."

"Nice."

"But I appreciate this, Blair. More than you know." The smile was replaced by worry lines across her forward as she stared at the notebook.

46

"When did you open this place? Last time I was here this was a paddock," he said.

"Even back then I had an application in with council to build the shop and house. It took a few nail-biting months to be approved." Her eyes met his again. "Nan left me some money. Not millions, but enough to build the shop. I've been saving since my first job when I was still at school and was able to borrow enough for the house and to set up the inside of this place. Not cheap with all the plumbing and the equipment."

"That's a lot to take on alone, Miranda. I'm in awe."

Her eyebrows lifted for an instant. Did she think he was being smart? But then those worry creases returned.

"Thanks. Up until August I still groomed out of the shed up at Pop's place. And I've been growing every week since, but if I'm out of action for too long . . ." Her hand touched the notebook. "I did the sums and there's not much wiggle room."

A car drove into the carpark and Miranda looked past Blair. "Cappy is here." She carefully stood. "Tash won't be far away."

"Would you like me to help out for a bit?"

"I'm fine. Really. But before Cappy comes in; we never discussed if you want to be paid each day or just once you finish up?" Miranda shuffled to the end of the counter, holding it for support.

"Later is fine. I don't mind hanging around for a while."

Why does this matter so much to me?

She shook her head. "Seriously, no. But you'll be back in the morning?"

"Wouldn't miss those pooches for anything."

He'd been dismissed. There was no other way to describe it. Miranda didn't want him helping apart from taking over the dog walking. By the time he'd left after finishing his coffee—at least she'd let him stay long enough for that!—Tash had arrived and was making a big fuss of Miranda. The last thing he'd heard was Tash ordering Miranda to stay behind the counter until she'd washed Cappy and could take over.

At least she listens to someone.

Seeing how capable her assistant was made Blair feel a little better about heading home. A big, mud-splattered 4WD was parked out the front of Kane's house and he was climbing out of the back of it with a sleeping bag in his hand. This he tossed onto a pile including a tent, tarps, and an esky. All were as muddy as the vehicle.

"Did you get caught in a mudslide?"

Kane stopped unpacking and ran a hand through his hair. Muddy hair. "What have you done to my house?"

"Made it festive. What have you done to your . . . well, everything? Even your neck has mud splatters."

"Clients. Clients who think they know better than their guide and park where they were told not to and then get their wheels spinning before I can get them out of trouble. Anyway, give me a hand?"

They pitched the tent and laid out the sleeping bag and tarps and Kane spent a couple of minutes spraying them down with water funnelled through a high-pressure hose from one of the half dozen tanks around the property. He did the same to the 4WD to get the worst of the mud off and clear the number plates. The sun would dry everything. Blair took the esky inside and told Kane to shower while he unpacked it.

That done, he cooked them both breakfast.

"I usually eat before dawn." Kane was in the doorway,

drying his hair and back in clean clothes. "So that smells particularly good."

"Figured you'd been making mud pies instead of breakfast." Blair laughed at his joke.

"Yeah. Nah. Don't give up your day job." He disappeared again.

Blair stared at the eggs in the pan. His day job was his dream job. But if he lost it tomorrow, he'd simply go and get something similar. Miranda, on the other hand, was fighting for hers. Fighting for the livelihood and career she was carving out, not through university studies and a couple of breaks, but sheer hard work, determination, and talent. All self-taught.

"Says a lot about her."

"About who? And those need to come out of the pan, dude."

Time to stop thinking aloud.

Over eggs and toast and coffee, Blair filled Kane in on the events since last night. "I wish she'd let me help a bit more. That ankle will be killing her tonight."

"From the sound of it, Miranda's quite able to manage."

"I've worked with footballers who listened better than she does."

Kane threw his head back and laughed.

"What?"

"Dude, have you never spent time with a woman? Do you not get how tough they are? I'd bet she's worked out how to keep grooming and run her salon and do enough to manage the pain. She doesn't need some guy telling her to slow down."

"Yeah but I'm not just some guy, Kane."

Fork halfway to his mouth, Kane paused, a slight smile on his face. Actually, smirk was the word for it.

You think I'm sweet on her.

"We've been besties forever. You know that."

"Good foundation for a relationship."

Almost spitting out the mouthful he'd just taken, Blair reached for his coffee, glaring at his brother. This wasn't a relationship. Not that kind anyway. Kane was openly grinning as he tucked into his breakfast.

At this rate, Blair would return the Christmas gift he'd purchased for Kane. And remove all the decorations.

There is no relationship.

Chapter Ten

Much as she wanted to go to Pop's tonight, the idea of trekking all the way up to his house on foot made her ankle hurt without even moving. She could have driven up—thank goodness she had an automatic car—but there was the matter of the steps to his door. He'd been down to check on her twice during the day and now, the appearance of Tangles bounding through the open back door alerted her to his third visit.

"Hey doggie." She scratched behind Tangles's ears as his warm brown eyes regarded her. "I know. I've not given you any attention for ages."

"But *I* have so don't let him fool you." Pop carried a baking dish covered in foil which he placed onto the counter before closing the door. "And he's eaten."

"Thank you. And for bringing dinner."

Pop turned the oven on then sat at the table opposite Miranda. She had another chair pulled out and her foot was on it.

"Hurting?"

"Yup. But not so much I can't get around a bit. Blair

suggested crutches but I'm worried I'll frighten a dog if I'm using them."

"Doesn't stop you having them for outside work hours."

"I'll think about it."

"Or I can dig up my walking stick."

Pop was joking but the idea had merit. Easier to walk with one than learn to manage crutches.

Tangles stood at the back door and waited. Pop pushed himself up and shuffled over to open it for him. "What did you forget to do, young man?" He left the door open and put the baking dish into the oven. "What are you doing on that?"

'That' was the laptop.

"Paying bills. Kind of sad seeing how quickly my business account depletes thanks to taking care of invoices from suppliers."

Not just sad. Scary.

She pointed to one line. "My account for this supplier was three times higher than a month ago!"

He peered over her shoulder. "Pet treats?"

"Almost every customer buys at least one. Some are even coming back each week and I ordered more than normal to account for people stocking up when I'm closed, but even so . . ."

"But they're selling, kiddo. Which means you *can* pay your bills. And, in turn, means you are doing things right."

The pride in his voice should have reassured Miranda. Instead, there was a lump in her throat. He'd be proud of her no matter what and it did mean a lot to hear his confidence but there were so many 'what ifs' that her head spun.

"Hey. You look like you want to cry. Is it the ankle? I can get you some ice or something—"

She shook her head. "Not my ankle. I'm a bit worried, Pop."

"Can you turn that thing off?"

She closed the laptop and pushed it away. Tangles trotted back in and sat at her side. The more she stroked his soft fur, the more the stress eased.

"Do you know what worry is, child?" Pop pulled a chair around closer and took one of her hands in his. "Worry is an unresolved problem. Best way to resolve it is taking action. Now, action doesn't mean running all over the place, which is just as well given your state." He grinned. "No marathons for a while. However, working out what you can't control is every bit as important as knowing what you can fix."

Worry is an unresolved problem.

"When did you get so wise, Pop?"

"Long story."

"I see." She took a deep breath. "Okay. I can't fix the fact that for a short time I'm less mobile than usual. I can't do dog walking. Nor can I stand and serve in the shop all day."

"So what solutions have you come up with to work around these restrictions?"

"Blair has taken over the dog walking. He's managing two clients every morning which is a total of seven dogs. I won't take on any further walking clients until I'm recovered."

Pop nodded.

"Tash and I spoke at length about ways to make the most of our time each day. I've closed the bookings, so no more squeezing in another dog before Christmas. We shuffled a few dogs around so that all the bathing is done in the morning and I look after customers, then Tash takes over the shop in the afternoon, which is tending to be the busiest time. It isn't ideal but it is short term and everyone has been really nice and understanding."

Maybe I've done more than I realised.

"Sounds as though you've got a lot under control. So why the worry?"

Miranda bit her bottom lip hard. This emotional state must be a lingering response to the shock of the fall. And tiredness.

"What does Blair have to say?" he asked.

"Blair? Well, he's offered to spend more time here to lend a hand, which is sweet, but I can't accept. He's home to visit his brother and other friends. Plus, if he hadn't seen me fall, he would have been none the wiser."

Pop patted her shoulder as he got up. "Good thing he was. And for what it's worth? Blair Maxwell is a good person and if he offers again, I'd accept. What have you got to lose by letting him help?"

Those words haunted Miranda over the next couple of days. Every morning Blair wandered through the back door ready to collect what was needed for the dog walking clients. An hour or so later he'd return everything and bring her a coffee. He'd hang around until she got busy, then head off. He hadn't offered to help again and she was pleased not to have to refuse. This arrangement was working well and had taken a weight off her shoulders.

But by night, when she limped around the shop locking doors, turning off lights, and fixing shelves, Pop's words would circle her mind.

What do I have to lose?

She knew the answer and wasn't happy about it. Pride kept her from accepting help. She'd been this way her whole life. Somewhere deep inside was a barrier which rose when she ran into a big problem. Solving it was her job. Finding a way to manage a situation without impacting anyone else. Almost everything she had was through her hard work and it felt wrong to expect other people to dive in if she fell short. And she had no idea why she was like this.

Tonight all she wanted was dinner and an early night. Tangles was with her and she fed him and left him to his own devices outside while she took a salad from the fridge. Pop kept bringing meals and usually staying for dinner but there was a note on the bowl.

Catching up with a friend tonight so will eat out. Phone me if you need anything. Pop.

For some strange reason the image of that slice of decadent chocolate cake in his fridge the other day popped into her head. Was he seeing a . . . woman?

Miranda laughed at the silly thought. Pop was not only quite elderly but had been devoted to Nan. He had plenty of friends and was probably playing darts at the pub. It was good for him to stay socially active. The couple of times he'd wandered from home had frightened her, which was why she'd panicked the other night when he wasn't at home. He'd been vague about his whereabouts. Just out for a walk. Or shopping, most recently. But nothing more to explain his absence, and although Miranda wasn't trying to keep tabs on her grandfather, she worried about his wellbeing.

Worry is an unresolved problem.

In this case, his occasional disappearances were the problem and, somehow, she needed to resolve it for her peace of mind.

Chapter Eleven

Sunday was everyone's day of rest. Kane had been home last night and slept in. The dogs had a day off their usual walk. And Bindarra Creek Pampered Pets was closed for the day. Blair drove around to the back of the house.

Tangles ran up to him, tail wagging madly. He was a terrific dog, always happy to greet a visitor and such a wonderful companion for both Miranda and Pop Layton. Although he had to be heading toward ten years, he was in great shape thanks to the care he got.

"Where's Mum?"

"Mum? Haha. I'm over here."

"What are you doing?" Even as he spoke, he noticed the words had an accusatory tone. "I mean, shouldn't you be off your feet?"

"That wasn't much better." Miranda had dragged the anti-fatigue mats out from the salon onto a small concrete block. She held a broom, ready to clean them. "The place won't maintain itself, sadly. And I'm taking my time."

As if to prove her point, Miranda leaned on the broom and tilted her head. At least she was smiling.

When did you get so pretty?

Her eyes were the deepest blue and always expressive. Right now they were laughing at him.

"Er . . . how is the ankle?"

"It has its moments but I think the swelling is down a bit. Once I finish doing this I'll rest it for a bit before the next job."

"Or . . ." he grinned and held his hand out, "you could rest it now and boss me around for a while. Come on, let me practice my brooming skills."

"Brooming? Is that even a word?"

"Is now."

She was wavering but her grip on the broom was still tight. "Did you go to Carols by Candlelight last night?"

He shook his head. "Kane was home and we drove over to spend the evening with Mum and Dad. I take it you didn't?"

"Wanted to. Pop offered to take me but the week had caught up. Here, sweep these and then turn them over and sweep again." She pushed the broom at him. "I might sit for a minute."

Stunned, he almost missed the broom handle as it fell toward him. Miranda was already limping to a seat in the shade and Tangles followed. Once she sat, she raised both eyebrows. "Sweep, lacky. Standing around won't get you an iced tea when I allow you to have a break."

He chuckled and got on with it. This was the most relaxed Miranda had been since he'd come home and he'd forgotten how much he enjoyed her cheeky side. "How long have we been friends?"

"Forever. Why?"

"First time you've let me help without an argument. More or less."

She was quiet for a few minutes and when he glanced

over, wondering if he'd said the wrong thing, Miranda had a hand resting on Tangles's head but her eyes were closed. Was this why she'd given in so easily? She was exhausted.

As though feeling his scrutiny, her eyes opened. "Do you need supervision?"

He lay the broom down and went around the mats to where she sat. "Would you like some water or something?"

"This will sound silly . . ."

"Go on." He squatted in front of her.

"I missed your coffee this morning. Fully intended to make one with breakfast but it got to be a bit of an effort."

You missed the coffee . . . or me bringing you one?

She leaned toward him and her ponytail fell forward over her shoulder, her hair trailing the scent of lime as it swung. Close up, her features were drawn and a bit paler than usual, but her skin was flawless and her lips were . . .

"Shall I make us both a coffee? Or I could go buy some." His heart thudded. She'd better not see what he'd been thinking because then he might kiss her and no good could come of that. None at all.

She might tell me to leave forever.

There was something going on behind those eyes as she regarded him for long seconds. Then she sat back. "I'd love one. If you really don't mind making them?"

"Careful, Miranda," he said as he stood. "First the mats then the coffee? You're catching on to this 'letting people help you' thing."

She frowned. "Well, I can make the coffee."

"I'm teasing you. Since when do you take me seriously?"

He wasn't hanging around for the answer. Some things were best left unspoken.

After bringing their coffees out, Blair finished the mats. "Back in the salon?"

"Oh, I can move them."

"You have a hot coffee in your hand. Is the door unlocked to the shop?"

She nodded and settled back on her chair, watching as he lugged the heavy rubber mats inside. He put one in the bathing room, two in the grooming room beside the tables, and the last behind the counter. The floor was slightly damp from being mopped and everything in here was spotless.

No wonder you're tired.

An idea was forming as he went outside. "Do you have plans for the rest of the day? Once we finish things off here?"

Her cup was empty but he'd barely touched his. He sipped as he waited for a response. There couldn't be anything left to do.

"Well, I usually spend a few hours each Sunday updating the books and starting on the week's orders, but having to be in the shop rather than the salon so much has let me do a lot of those things between customers. And Pop is out this afternoon. Again."

"In that case, I know a little spot along the river which is perfect for a picnic. I can park within a couple of metres so all you need to do is manage a few steps."

"Why?"

"Why not?" This mattered. Blair hadn't worked out why, but it did. "How about I pick you up at one, and you and Tangles can relax near the river for a bit. Kane and I have a ton of leftovers at home so I'll toss a selection into an esky."

Her mouth was open, probably to refuse.

"What do you think, Tangles?" Blair asked.

The dog's tail thumped the ground.

"Yup, he agrees."

"Then who am I to say no? Do you want me to bring anything?"

"A sunhat."

Chapter Twelve

Until she dangled her bare feet into the cool river, Miranda hadn't realised how much stress she was carrying around.

The simple act of sitting on soft grass as water gently caressed her skin was pure bliss. Blair had removed the strapping from the sprained ankle and encouraged her to enjoy the water, promising to rebandage it later.

The beauty of having a sports physio around.

Tangles had jumped straight in for a swim and now was rolling around on the grass in the sunshine. Blair filled a bowl with water and left it in the shade for him.

"Hungry?" He'd spread out a picnic blanket and was unpacking an esky.

"Starving. Do you need a hand?"

"Nope. You stay there as long as you want. In fact, I can bring you a plate if you like and join you."

She shuffled to make it easier to see him. "I might want to keep all this sparkling water for myself."

"And I might want to keep all of this delicious food for—"

"Okay, okay. I'll share."

Something had changed today. Before Blair had

arrived at the house earlier, Miranda had become despondent about her mobility. Dragging the mats out had taken all of her energy and she'd had no idea whether she'd get them back inside, so how could she manage the coming week? Not only was the salon booked up, but the increase in customers to the shop showed no signs of slowing. All good things. Except she was struggling to cover the bases.

Hearing the car approach, Miranda had considered hiding in the house and pretending she wasn't there. But her car was parked in plain view. So she'd forced a smile and hoped he wouldn't stay long. Keeping up the appearance of holding things together was hard work.

He must have caught her at a moment of weakness because she'd never intended to give him the broom. Or let him tease her into dropping her guard. Sitting there while he worked was oddly calming, not at all as uncomfortable as she'd expected. And she'd almost gone to sleep.

"Anything you don't want?"

"Hm? Oh, no, you choose. Bonus points for cheese."

A minute or two later he handed her an overflowing plate and settled beside her. His own shoes were off and he lowered his feet into the river with a small sigh. "Nice."

Tangles wandered over and lay between them with a hopeful expression. Miranda picked a strip of carrot and offered it. "That really is all you're getting, mate. That or nothing."

He gently took the morsel and headed under a nearby tree to enjoy it.

"Meanie. He was hoping for a wrap with cheese and pickles."

"How many labradors do you know who are as fit and healthy as Tangles?"

Neatly folded to one side were two wraps which looked homemade and smelled fresh. Then there were all the filling options. Sliced hard cheese, spinach leaves, tomatoes, olives, what looked like caramelised onions, some pickle spears, and a dollop of relish. It took no time to construct a wrap using the accompanying fork and when she bit in, she closed her eyes.

Perfect.

"I can only take some of the credit. Kane made the wraps. And the relish. One day he'll make someone very happy," Blair said. "Great cook. Keeps a nice house. Usually friendly enough."

The last part made her laugh and then she almost choked on the rest of her mouthful. Blair grabbed bottled water and opened it. A few gulps later she was fine, but Tangles had trotted over and nudged her as if to check she was okay.

"Go back to the tree. I'm fine." She kissed the top of Tangles's nose. "So when is your brother going to find someone who is looking for a friendly enough husband?"

"He says he's too busy."

"I know that feeling."

She shoved more food in her mouth before she could say anything else so stupid. Being busy was an easy excuse to avoid accepting dates or letting well-meaning friends— or Pop—set her up. A boyfriend would distract her from growing her business. Most likely they'd want lots of her attention—more than she could give while she owed so much money and needed to create a sustainable income. So she'd wait. It wasn't important.

Blair stared at her.

Don't ask any questions. I'd like to stay relaxed.

"Speaking of Kane, he's hired a rock-climbing wall for the Christmas Eve town party at Lette Park. He hopes it will encourage some locals to book adventures with his company," Blair said.

Relieved about the change of subject, Miranda nodded. "I saw him advertising in the local paper. He needs better artwork though; his logo and stuff all got lost among the more professional ads. Sorry, I don't mean to be critical."

Blair made a note on his phone. "I'll mention it to him. No point spending money if he's missing the mark. Most of his clients are from out of town and keep him busy, but he thinks he's not reaching Bindarra Creek residents who don't realise he's offering more than a guided walk in the National Park."

The meal finished, Blair took their plates back to the esky and packed the remnants of food up, supervised by Tangles. He snuck another piece of carrot to the dog. Miranda smiled to herself and then reluctantly lifted her feet up out of the river. Standing was a different matter— without the strapping, her ankle wanted to buckle as she tested it.

"Wait on, Miranda." Blair was there in a few seconds and let her use him as a support. "Come and sit and I'll fix that right up."

From the car he collected a towel to dry her feet and a small bag. Inside was a range of tapes and bandages along with a few items Miranda didn't recognise. He extracted scissors and two types of tape plus a spray can.

She giggled. "Are you going to draw graffiti on me?"

Blair began shaking the can, grinning. There was something about his smile. Always had been. He was often so serious, and then the corners of his lips would lift and his eyes would sparkle. She'd rarely been able to stop herself responding in kind even if her mood was dark. He was so good looking and it was a wonder some Sydney girl hadn't snapped him up yet.

Unless someone has. What if he has a girlfriend?

What did it matter? He deserved happiness.

"I'll be gentle so there's no need for the worried look."

"No, I'm not worried about my ankle."

64

"Okay then, what?"

He carefully lifted her foot so that her calf rested on the top of his leg, the ankle free to attend to. "The way I do this is a little different from the doctor. I mean, he did a perfect job but this is how I manage sports injuries and it will allow a little more freedom of movement while still supporting the ankle."

First he sprayed her ankle and foot. Her toes curled with the cold.

"Just a type of adhesive. Then I use a soft tape underneath and finally the firmer one. Why were you looking worried?"

Head down as he worked, he couldn't have seen her puzzling over an answer, yet somehow he knew. "I'm an open book so if you want to ask something, go right ahead. It's about which is the most famous footballer I've worked with, isn't it?"

"Yeah, right. No, I wondered if you have someone special waiting for you in Sydney."

His face lifted in surprise and he shook his head. "Nobody. Why?"

Exactly, Miranda. Why? It is none of your business.

"Oh, no reason. Probably because we were talking about Kane before in that context."

Blair began cutting strips of tape. "If I move your foot to this position"—he tilted her toes upward a bit— "is that too uncomfortable?"

His touch was gentle. His skin against hers felt good. If only things were different. If there was more time. Her throat tightened. Blair would return to Sydney in a few days and it would be goodness knows how long until he came home again.

"Miranda?"

"Um, not uncomfortable."

Once he finished, he lowered her foot to the ground.

"Those are pretty waterproof so you can shower without using a plastic bag. Just watch in case the tape gets a bit ratty though. Would you like some more water?"

"I'm a bit tired."

"I'll take you home."

He pulled her to her feet and they were face to face.

"Shall we dance?" he murmured. His fingers caressed the skin of her arms and his eyes were unreadable. They were inches apart. He smelled good and she drifted a fraction closer.

So did he.

Her breath caught.

He's leaving soon.

She stepped back. "Do you mind if I go home now?"

If there was disappointment on his face, she didn't need to see it. It was all she could feel.

Chapter Thirteen

Everything had changed in an instant.

Miranda had been so happy. So relaxed and more like the person he'd known for so long once the stress of her business was on the back burner and her toes were in the river.

And then you had to wreck it.

He'd almost kissed her.

People didn't kiss their best friends.

Not the way he wanted to kiss Miranda.

For one heart-stopping moment she'd been in his arms and he'd been lost in her eyes. The moment was gone as fast as it came and she'd pulled away and asked to go home. All the way, she'd stared out of the window, her fingers laced together on her lap. She'd let him assist her to the door then without even meeting his eyes, mumbled a thanks for the picnic and that she'd see him in the morning. Then he'd left.

"At least she didn't fire you."

"Fire you?"

Blair jumped. He hadn't meant to speak aloud and

now Kane would take great delight in ribbing him about Miranda.

"What are you doing out here? Have a beer, mate." Kane handed him one and joined him leaning against the railing.

The sky was darkening with the coming of night and birds were settling into trees, squabbling and flapping around as they found their perches for the evening. Blair missed this in Sydney. He had an apartment around Bondi and most of the birds were seagulls. At least he could hear the ocean despite the fact that he couldn't afford a place with a view. This was different though, with the smell of the gums and the humidity lifting a bit with the night air.

"You didn't lose your job did you?"

"Neither of them."

"Neither? Oh." Kane had the expected smirk on his face when Blair glanced at his brother. "For a minute I thought you'd done something to upset your footie club boss. But it's Miranda. What did you do?"

"Nothing. Literally nothing."

"Were you meant to do something?"

"Let it go." Blair turned his back on the scenery and gulped a couple of mouthfuls.

"Impossible, little brother. You took her on a picnic. Now, the two of you have been besties since early high school. Always wished I'd had such a good relationship with a girl. They're often much better company than a man is, but every girl I tried to be friends with wanted more."

Blair burst into laughter.

Kane looked hurt—for a minute—then he joined in.

When Blair could get some words out it was to give as good as he got. "Mister Irresistible, aren't you?"

"I am. Fighting them off," Kane grinned.

"We talked about your love life, or lack thereof."

"Excuse me? You did what?"

"Yup. Miranda thought there'd be someone out there for you. Me? Not so sure."

Silence fell for a bit as they finished their beers. Kane was more than his big brother. They were friends. Always had been and, despite Kane's far more serious approach to life, Blair loved him to bits. Didn't stop him having some fun at Kane's expense, of course.

Kane stared at him.

Blair shrugged. "What?"

"How is life in Sydney? Really. I enjoy the emails and texts about all the stuff you *want* me to see— pictures of Bondi Beach, clips of the players you've worked with, a trip on a Manly ferry—which is cool, by the way. But is it what you expected?"

Searching for an answer, Blair dropped onto one of the rattan chairs against the wall, facing back out to the front paddock. Kane followed.

"Yes and no. I love what I do. Love being a physio. And there are some awesome people where I work."

"And I hear a "but"."

Everyone thought Blair was a drifter at heart. He'd gone from job to job while at university, bored quickly and wanting the next challenge. But he'd stuck through his years of education and training.

"I miss you. And Mum and Dad. I miss Bindarra Creek. Perhaps I'm a country boy at heart and, although the city is very, very exciting at times, nothing beats this."

His phone beeped a message and his heart skipped a beat.

But it was one of his mates in town wanting to catch up tomorrow. He quickly replied, then turned the phone off. If Miranda decided she didn't want him there tomorrow then she could tell him face to face.

"Blair. What's upset you tonight? I'm not going to tease you."

"I think I'm feeling more than friendship for Miranda. And it's clear she isn't interested. You know, I enjoy helping her. Being there for her. But she's so stubborn and we had . . . well, almost a moment today. But then she wanted to go home and said just about nothing."

Go on. Laugh at me.

Kane patted his shoulder. "That sucks."

After blinking in surprise at the supportive response, Blair nodded. "Yeah. But all the way back from her place all I could think about was not losing her as a friend. She matters to me a lot and if I need to forget about . . . something more, well then that's a small price to pay."

Much later, as he lay in bed staring at the ceiling, he knew it wasn't true. Somehow, in just a few days, he'd managed to fall in love with his best friend.

Chapter Fourteen

"Can you believe how busy we are already?" Tash dashed through the front door after carrying a couple of bags of goodies out for a customer. "I need to wash dogs, so will you be okay?"

Miranda had opened the front door early to let a grooming client in and since then a steady stream of customers had been in. Many were simply browsing, curious about what gift ideas they'd find. But Tash had been running back and forth to save Miranda's ankle.

We can't go on like this.

"Yes, go wash."

Tash disappeared into the bathing room.

Her ankle was a bit better today, thanks to the way Blair bandaged it yesterday. But walking hurt. He'd asked how it felt when he'd dropped the dog-walking gear back earlier and offered, in an offhand fashion, to hang around to help. Like he did every day. Except he hadn't returned with coffees. And he'd driven off when she got caught up with the first customer.

Which is what he should do. Let it go, Miranda!

It was a mammoth effort to push down feelings which had messed with her sleep and forced her up extra early this morning. And as two cars drove in, she lifted her chin and told herself to stop thinking about it. There'd be time later to work through it all. Much later.

Another dog was dropped in; thank goodness a regular just in for a bath and nails. Tash had things in hand and glanced up with a smile from the hydro bath as Miranda hobbled past with the dog. He happily went into the pen and climbed straight onto the raised bed, knowing the routine well after visiting so often.

A young woman in gym gear waited for Miranda at the counter, nails drumming on the top. "Oh, you *are* here. I need a big bag of my usual food." She shoved her loyalty card at Miranda. "I'll pay first then go and open the boot."

"I'll just go and get a trolly for it and—"

"If it's too much trouble I can shop elsewhere."

People were always friendly in the shop. *Always*. But the woman glaring at Miranda was clearly having a bad day. With a plastered-on smile, Miranda rang up the sale. "Nothing is too much trouble. All part of the service."

The woman made a humphing sound as she hurried out.

"Hope you don't mind waiting." Miranda muttered under her breath as she picked up the offending bag. She was used to lugging these twenty kilo bags around—lighter than the feed bags for the cattle—but once it was up on her shoulder she struggled to walk. By the time she shuffled out of the door, the woman had her hands on her hips and a scowl on her face.

The carpark was only a few metres away but might as well have been on the moon. Halfway there, her ankle throbbing, she knew she'd have to put the bag down for a minute.

"I really don't have all day!"

Blair appeared from beyond the woman's car carrying two coffees. He glanced at the woman and Miranda then put the coffees on the ground and sprinted across, taking the bag. "Not a word."

Did you just wink at me?

"Now, is this fine here next to your gym bag?" His voice was cheery as he lowered the bag into the car. "I reckon these dogfood bags would be a perfect workout! Miranda keeps fit carrying them around but her sprained ankle doesn't approve of extra weight at the moment."

"Oh. You should have said you were injured." The woman's face reddened as she glanced at Miranda. "Sorry. Christmas stress."

"All good. Merry Christmas," Miranda replied.

Blair collected the coffees and joined Miranda as the car left. "Like a lift? I've already warmed up carrying the bag."

She snorted and started back to the shop.

"Do you have a trolley for such big items?" he asked.

"She wouldn't wait for me to get one. Told me she'd shop elsewhere."

"And there I was being so pleasant to her. Is Tash not here?"

Miranda stopped suddenly and gazed up at Blair, shading her eyes from the sun. "*Tash* is busy. If I could wash dogs sitting down I'd swap places but for now we're doing our best. Most people are kind. She"—she gestured toward the front gate— "was rude. Anyway, thanks for taking the bag. Did you forget something?"

The only response from Blair was the lifting of his eyebrows.

She knew she sounded abrupt and cross. That woman might have had Christmas stress but Miranda had the weight of the world on her.

He raised the coffees and the faintest of smiles flickered across his mouth.

It was annoying to feel her own lips responding in kind.

"The coffee shop was busy when I went past this morning so I doubled back. I have a spare arm if you'd like?"

Nope. No more touching you.

"I'll follow. No running today, just a slow trudge."

"Then we'll be slow together."

He was behaving as if nothing had happened . . . as if nothing had *almost* happened, yesterday. Had she imagined the moment between them? Hopefully. She had no intention of losing her best friend over a misunderstood feeling.

The coffee was just what she needed but only half a cup got drunk thanks to another wave of customers. She came back to the counter with some dog bowls for a customer to find Blair serving someone, chatting away as he deftly rang up a sale. About to say something, she clamped her lips shut. His customer was smiling as Blair suggested they add a few extra treats and by the time they left with their box of products, the sale had doubled in value.

When she was able to finish her coffee it was almost cold. Blair was helping someone put their dog into a car after grooming.

"Is he working here this week?" Tash helped herself to one of the tills—which was controlled by a computer system—and updated the file of the dog which she'd just finished.

"No. Any idea how he knew the password to the system?"

"I gave him mine." Tash suddenly looked up, eyes round. "Oh, was I not meant to? He said you were with someone and I figured he'd forgotten his."

Miranda didn't know whether to thank Blair or yell at him, but she could never be cross with Tash. "You did nothing wrong. But he doesn't work here apart from the dog walking. I guess he wanted to help in a busy moment."

"Well, he should. Work here, that is. Think how much easier it would be for you."

"I'm managing."

Tash's expression said otherwise but she muttered, "Yes, boss," and returned to what she'd been doing.

Yes, boss?

That was new.

Blair was whistling to himself as he sauntered back in. The shop was free of customers again and he pulled product forward on a shelf.

"You don't need to do that, Blair."

Tash grabbed her clipboard and hightailed it for the washing room.

"I like making it look nice." He kept tidying the shelf as he walked then stopped in front of the counter. "What?"

"What? Um . . . you don't work here."

Blair shrugged.

"No really. Look, I appreciate your help earlier but since when do you know how to handle a till? That point of sale system is pretty new to the market and—"

"And is easy to use. I looked over your shoulder a couple of times. Just couldn't work out your password." He crossed his arms and his eyes narrowed. "I've overstepped."

"I can't afford another staff member right now, not even for a few days. And Tash and I are managing."

Just by the skin of our teeth.

"I see."

His tone was identical to Tash's 'yes, boss'. And it irked.

"No, you don't see. I have a sprained ankle—that is all. My brain works, my selling skills are brilliant, grooming is still doable, I can do just about everything except carry big, heavy items." Everyone thought she was weak. Useless. "I built this place. Well, not personally, but I paid for it. Designed it. Chose everything you see. Which makes me proud of what I've done so far. But I need income to pay for it all and I can't squeeze out any more—"

Blair came around the counter and took her hands. It only made her more upset and she pulled them away, furious at herself when his eyes gave away his hurt. Why did he even bother with her? Tears prickled at the back of her eyes and she bit down on her bottom lip to give herself something else to feel.

"I haven't asked to be paid. Miranda, I have contracted employment which is paying me even during my holidays . . . more money than I know what to do with."

That really doesn't help.

"You're my best friend and all I see is someone struggling—"

"I'm not struggling!" The words came out louder than she meant. "I'm just injured at a really bad time."

"And injured people need a chance to recover. All I want is to give you a hand so you can."

Before the first stupid tears fell she turned away. "I'm not one of your footballers, Blair. I don't have a million dollars lying around to cover expenses while I recuperate. It might be your world now but it isn't mine."

He sighed deeply. A frustrated sigh. "Okay, I get that I'm upsetting you being here, so I'll go. And I'll see you in the morning."

She nodded, willing him to leave before she embarrassed herself.

"Just think about it though. Heck, I don't care if you

76

want to barter for my help if it sits better with you, because there's got to be some middle ground where we can meet. The offer stands."

Miranda didn't move until she heard his car drive out.

I won't cry. And I won't give up.

Chapter Fifteen

There was no time to feel sorry for herself. The morning flew past between customers, dogs, and the phone. People desperate to book their dog in before Christmas. Others wanting to know the opening hours of the shop and whether she was doing a late night.

"Honestly, Tash. I had no clue how much interest the shop would have or I'd have planned better. I just hope the deliveries arrive on time."

"Well, we are pretty awesome here." Tash grinned as she went past to greet another customer. "Go and clip now."

"You've not had lunch."

"My sandwich is behind the counter. Go."

It helped to sit for a while and focus on nothing other than the gorgeous little poodle who'd become a favourite client. Every visit she was the same sweet girl who enjoyed smooches and came out looking like a million dollars. Once she'd given her one last kiss on the nose, Miranda popped her into her pen and gave her a treat.

She went out to ask Tash to phone the poodle's owner and stopped in her tracks at the store filled with people.

Tash had several in a line and was progressively working her way through them, cheerily thanking people for their patience as she rang up their purchases. The poodle's owner was browsing in the corner of the shop, arms full with a bed.

"Let me pop that behind the counter and I'll collect—"

"Yes love, you take that and can you show me that brush you mentioned the last time? I also need shampoo for in-between visits. Oh, and some treats."

By the time she'd looked after the customer and brought her doggie out, Tash was back from a trip to the carpark. "Let me put all your lovely products into the bed and I'll bring this to the car for you."

Finally able to do what she'd come out for, Miranda checked the schedule and was about to return to the salon when a movement caught her eye. The shop wasn't empty after all.

"Hello there. How can I help today?"

The man mustn't have heard her as he didn't respond but kept staring at the stand of dog toys. She was almost at his side before he noticed, and jumped. "Didn't see you there."

"Sorry to surprise you. What kind of dog toy interests you?"

"Something squeaky. A ball? For Copper. My, uh . . . friend's cattle dog."

Miranda picked out two balls of the right size for the breed and handed them to him. "Test them. Go on, it's the best way to choose. Both are really high bouncers and the one in your left hand also floats."

He squeezed both and they squawked. "This one." He held up the left and returned the other one to its hook.

"Excellent. What else would you like? I bet Copper would enjoy beef jerky. Very popular." She led Heath toward the treats. "If it's for Christmas, we just made these little gift packs." Miranda offered a cellophane-wrapped assortment of beef jerky, beef liver pieces, and beef tendons, tied with a pretty green bow. "Lots there to keep everyone happy on Christmas Day."

Another nod. It seemed like that was all he wanted, and he headed to the counter.

Tash ran back in. "I'll ring those up."

With a grateful smile, Miranda left Tash with the customer and returned to the salon. She was miles behind. There were three more dogs to clip. She was starving. And her ankle reminded her with every step that she was doing too much. Her heart sank as her earlier thoughts returned.

We really, really can't go on like this.

"I wish I was younger, kiddo. I can manage a couple of hours a day but then need a rest." Pop sighed heavily. "Why don't you leave that for morning?"

Miranda was restocking the shelves. Most of the lights were out and she had a trolley filled with products she was progressively unpacking. "Maybe. I'll just do the toys. But don't wait for me if you want to eat." She slid replacement balls onto a hook. "And I don't want you in the shop, Pop. Ha, that rhymes."

"You think I'd drive customers away?"

He didn't sound too offended but she stopped and gave him a smile.

"Not even close. You helped so much before Tash came to work here, but you were on your feet too much and I know it hurt your hips. Most of the time Tash and I manage perfectly." She picked up some plush toys. "We have a good system but this coming week is shaping up to be crazy busy and the biggest problem is this stupid ankle of mine."

"Which you've been on all day. Come on, leave the trolley and sit for a bit. I want to see you eat."

He was right. She would set her alarm for half an hour earlier and finish in the morning.

Pop went ahead while she turned off the remaining lights and slowly made her way to the door connecting to her home. There, she glanced back. How pretty the shop was with the tinsel sparkling off the changing lights on the Christmas tree. Every customer deserved a good experience and her being stubborn worked against that.

It was well after nine when Pop left. He'd insisted on washing up so she could keep her foot elevated and had let Tangles out for a run. She locked up and headed for a shower. With water pouring over her head, drowning out all but the thoughts which refused to quiet down, the tears came.

Tears for the ankle pain that wouldn't leave her, even in bed.

Tears for the fear she wouldn't manage.

And tears of acceptance. If she intended to meet the needs of her customers then she needed help.

Tangles settled into his bed beside hers with a deep, contented sigh.

"I wish I was as carefree, doggo."

She climbed into bed, almost sighing to herself at the comfort of cool sheets and pillows. But she couldn't sleep yet. She sent a text to Blair.

Are you still awake?

He'd always been a night owl. Loved being awake when the rest of the world slept, but maybe the demands of his job in Sydney had changed his patterns. Her phone dinged.

Sure am. Want me to call?

"Not really." What if she cried again?

No, just wondered if that offer still stands?

She gazed at the screen. Nothing. Not even the little moving dots that meant he was writing a message. She added another line of text.

I can't pay. Not yet, but I will as soon as I have some extra. If that's okay?

Might as well give him an easy way out.

Another ding. She released the breath she hadn't realised she was holding.

No.

"What? But . . ." Her stomach churned as a second message appeared.

No need to pay me. I noticed a small cat product area and would love to take advantage of a generous staff discount to put together some gifts for Mum and Dad's cats. If that works for you?

Her shoulders relaxed.

You are most welcome to choose anything at cost price. Plus I have a box of cat products some suppliers gave me which I'm not going to stock. Those are free if you'd like them.

Bartering, he'd said. It still didn't feel like a fair swap.

Sounds good. I'll see you in the morning for dog-walking duty.

He added a little walking dog and she smiled.

Followed by shop assistant duty.

The image she sent back was of a shopping trolley.

Which reminded her she needed to shop for Christmas. Dropping her head back onto her pillows, she gazed at the ceiling. When would there be a chance to do that? No doubt Pop had got a lot already but even so . . .

Another message.

Sleep well.

She would.

You too.

Snuggling under the sheet, she yawned and closed her eyes. For once she could rest knowing not everything was on the shoulders of her small team.

Chapter Sixteen

This retail stuff was fun.

Second day working in the shop and Blair had a routine going. Walk the dogs first, picking up coffees on his return. Help unpack any deliveries and restock shelves. Check dogs in for grooming—he loved that bit because he got to play with them. And be alert for customers coming in.

Customers are key.

Miranda had said so half a dozen times yesterday while she ran through the basics. He agreed, of course. Excellent customer service was what made a small business stand out. The little shop was a picture and, from what he'd picked up so far, Miranda's choice of products was in line with the needs of those coming in for grooming, as well as hitting the right notes with curious browsers.

"You've done a brilliant job," he said.

"Thank you." Miranda settled on the stool and began tapping information into the computer about the dog she'd just groomed. "But it was only a standard tidy up."

"Oh, the dog. Nah. The shop."

She glanced up. "It is just a little pet supplies shop. Nothing unusual."

He leaned against the counter, eyes roving. Small it might be, but it was well planned out. One wall had petfood stands with a fridge and freezer at the end. The opposite wall was timber shelving holding dog beds and other large items. There was a window display area where the Christmas tree currently held court, surrounded by some gift ideas. A dozen small, four-sided stands were dotted throughout the floor space, each dedicated to a different product or species type.

"It is functional though." Miranda stood. "Are you going okay? No problems with customers?"

"Not one. You and Tash seem ahead of the game today."

A smile lit her face. "We are, thanks to you. But I have two more to clip so it is back to work for me."

She was walking a little better today as she made her way back to the main grooming room. From the shop, anyone could watch the dogs being groomed, thanks to big windows instead of walls.

"It is brilliant," he murmured.

And so is your smile.

There was no time to dwell on Miranda's smile and what it did to him. Customers were heading in and it was a group of two women with four children. And a gorgeous cattle dog . . . Was that Gypsy?

"Emma, Samantha. How nice to see you. And the family."

Emma Sullivan carried a baby while Samantha's children—twin boys at the toddling stage and little girl maybe four—immediately began exploring the shop.

"Hands in your pockets," Samantha Morgan told them. "Since when do you work here, Blair?"

Blair squatted to talk to the cattle dog, who was more

84

than happy to have the back of her ears scratched. "Just helping out for a few days while I'm back for Christmas."

"Ah. Helping *Miranda* out."

The women exchanged a glance.

Great.

"She sprained her ankle the other day. Anyway, how can I help today?"

Impressed with his ability to change the subject, Blair helped choose a toy for Gypsy, removed one small child from on top of cat furniture, retrieved half a dozen balls from under stands and a gift card 'posted' into a cat igloo, and signed both families up to the shop's loyalty program.

"Do you have any idea about rabbits?" Samantha asked at the counter.

Only that Mum used to complain about them eating her veggie garden.

"Hmm. Specifically?"

"We're thinking about getting one as a pet, but Miranda doesn't sell pets from the look of things."

"No, just all the good stuff for them. Let me ask."

Miranda was singing to a cocker spaniel as she clipped its coat. Blair's heart couldn't take much more of this newfound appreciation for every wonderful quality she had. The way the dog was relaxed, its tail wagging as she kept a sweet melody . . . Who sings to dogs?

"What's up?" She flicked off the clippers and glanced through the window to the shop. "Why are Samantha and Emma staring at us?"

"Probably never seen a groomer in action. Let alone a singing groomer. Anyway, Samantha wants to get a rabbit for the kids."

"Ah. Under the counter is a folder titled "referrals". In it there are a couple of local breeders as well as a rabbit and guinea pig shelter. Just put the details onto a card but remind them to come back here to buy what they need."

Is there anything you haven't thought of?

A few minutes later the families drove out of the carpark and Blair checked the shop again for any misplaced items. If someone didn't nominate Bindarra Creek Pampered Pets for a business award then he would. Miranda might be young and struggling to make ends meet, but she had everything to be proud of. And the local community was loving what she'd created.

"I can manage if you need to be at the shop." Kane didn't glance up as he deftly diced an onion then threw it into a frying pan. It joined half a dozen vegetables already sizzling with garlic and herbs and he had filleted a fish earlier to join them in the last few minutes of cooking.

"When did you get time to go and fish?"

"Early. On the way back from looking at Lette Park to see what I have to prepare for."

"Oh, the Christmas Eve party? No, I said I'll give you a hand with the climbing rock and am quite looking forward to having a crack myself."

Kane shot him a look. 'It isn't a toy for you to play with."

"Then who else will clip twenty dollar notes up there for anyone who reaches the top?"

Cutting completed, Kane cleaned up his work area. "That is sheer brilliance. Who gave you that idea?"

"What . . . you don't think I have my own brilliant ideas?" Blair loved this kind of banter. It was their relationship to a tee. He collected two beers from the fridge and opened them. "If you must know, a friend in the city is from the States. No idea how it came up but she was reciting the funniest story of a fair where someone did the

86

money thing and although nobody made it to the top, the climbing wall was the most popular place to be."

Kane straightened and stared at him. "A friend?"

"Funny thing… when a person meets other people in a social environment, they sometimes get on really well and enjoy others' company."

"As in . . . a friend?"

Blair felt his eyes roll. "Erin is a friend."

"Just checking."

"Maybe if you made some friends you'd understand."

"I have plenty of friends. Now, the climbing rock comes with two attendants which leaves me free to give demonstrations, help those who are a bit timid, and hopefully gain some new customers. If you can be a spotter and help with harnesses and the like?"

"In return for a climb."

"In return for as many climbs as you want." Kane grinned. "In between climbers of course. Ready for me to cook?"

"Haven't eaten since breakfast so yes, please. Can I help?"

"Set the table. Is the shop that busy?"

"Tash had a new dog in who didn't appreciate bath time plus he weighed about fifty kilos so I went and fed him treats after getting him into the bath." And avoided being nipped when the dog had had enough. "I reckon some owners have no idea about getting their pets used to grooming and then they expect the poor groomer to deal with a nervous or scared dog."

He rubbed the arm where teeth had met his shirt, not making an impression as the dog seemed to realise what he was doing and had controlled himself. Dogs were incredible. So smart.

Over dinner, which was delicious, talk turned to Christmas Day.

"Mum and Dad would like us there for lunch." Kane chased a piece of fish around his plate. "Any ideas for presents?"

"Lots of cat products. Turns out I know someone who has a good supply at a decent price." He laughed. There were a few things he had his eye on. "What about a new cat tree big enough for both the cats, plus a couple of cat igloos? And I can fill those with toys and treats."

"They'd love that. Those kitties are everything to them. And their outdoor area. I've been thinking about buying a vertical garden for herbs and stuff."

"Excellent idea. Mum mentioned she misses having the big veggie beds but there isn't the space in their new home." Blair added some more salad to his plate. "So we'll go over mid-morning and come back mid-afternoon?"

"No need to hurry back I wouldn't think," Kane said. Then he looked up. "Oh."

"Oh?"

"I see."

Blair shook his head. "Wish I did. As usual you're making no sense."

Finished, Kane neatly placed his knife and fork on the plate. "Nothing wrong with wanting to spend some time on Christmas Day with Miranda."

"I already spend every day with her. Christmas is for families." Blair got to his feet and collected both their plates, surprised by the sharpness in his tone. "Sorry. I just think she'd prefer to spend the day with her grandfather rather than put up with me. She really isn't comfortable having me help out."

"Miranda would feel that way with anyone. You won't know if she wants to spend any Christmas time with you unless you ask. So why not ask?"

With his back to his brother as he ran water into the sink, Blair had no answer. He had this silly vision in his head of sitting with Miranda and Pop Layton over Christmas dinner with laughter and conversation. Being around her away from work. Sharing special moments.

Except he'd be leaving again soon. Back to his new life. Leaving her to keep growing her new life. Asking for more was unfair.

To Miranda? Or to me?

Chapter Seventeen

"Are you certain today is Friday? I mean, Christmas Eve's eve?" Tash zipped up her grooming apron. "We've almost made it."

Her smile made Miranda smile back. And then hug the younger woman.

"I couldn't have done it without you. Any of it. Today and then just a few hours tomorrow and you can take a well-earned break."

Tash squeezed her tightly then stepped back as the phone rang. "We could fit one more dog in."

"No. We cannot. You get started and I'll be there shortly." Miranda answered the phone call, which fortunately was not a grooming hopeful but someone asking the opening hours. Blair wandered in as she hung up and she glanced at her watch.

"Whoops, I'm late," he said, clearly not the least bit concerned.

Can't expect you to keep to my hours when I don't even pay you.

"It *is* your last day with this company following a long and illustrious career. From a lowly start many years ago you've risen through the ranks to a place of respect and privilege." Miranda spread her arms wide and rotated slowly. "Is there even one corner of this esteemed establishment you've not improved by your particular talents? Over there, a perfectly placed bag of dog food. And there, the magnificence of the display of dog beds is proof of your value to Bindarra Creek Pampered Pets."

By now Blair had reached the other side of the counter where he stood with a coffee in each hand. His eyes twinkled and the corners of his mouth twitched up as she continued.

"Today is all about you, revered employee, so time does not matter. Take a long lunch; no doubt my personal assistant and private chef have laid out a five course meal in the dining hall. And then when you choose to depart, go knowing your absence will be felt and your parting will leave us bereft of your wisdom."

He placed the coffees on the counter. "In that case, may I request a raise?"

She waved her hands. "Your request will be considered." Then she glanced past him. "Show me your worth with the incoming clients."

With a giggle she could no longer contain, Miranda helped herself to a coffee and made her way to the salon. She sneaked a look through the window. Blair was already greeting the customer she'd seen heading in, an elderly lady who beamed up at him.

This really was his last day.

Her shoulders dropped.

He'd made a difference.

The customer said something to Blair and he burst into laughter. He'd made the customer comfortable with hardly any effort. Just his genuine friendliness and that gorgeous smile.

Which belongs in Sydney with the rest of him.

She had work to do.

The shop was busier today than Miranda had ever seen. Ever. So many people looking for last minute gifts and some of the shelves were empty. Blair was doing an excellent job of selling whatever was left and when there was a small break between grooming appointments, Miranda collected more products to quickly transform into gift packs.

Blair carried a large bag of dogfood out to the carpark with a customer, leaving the shop empty for the first time in hours. Tash was on an early lunch as they waited for the next dog to arrive. There was quiet. Even the couple of dogs waiting for pickup were asleep.

Perched on her stool at the counter, Miranda dropped her head onto folded arms for a moment. Tiredness racked her body and the need to rest almost hurt. Earlier, she'd served a couple of young women she'd been at school with. Same year level although not friends as such. They chatted about their big plans with their boyfriends and how tiring the week had been with endless parties. All she could think of was how different their lives were to hers. She had big responsibilities and the headaches that came with them.

I'd love to party. Dance away the stress.

But she'd never been one to do that. Anyway, with a sprained ankle, dancing was a dream for now.

Footsteps approached and her head shot up. She couldn't let customers see her like this!

"Go take a proper break, Miranda. Have lunch." It was only Blair, who was smiling but in a kind way, not laughing at her resting.

On queue her stomach rumbled. "Just for ten minutes. As long as you're sure?"

"No customers here."

Over his shoulder she saw a car drive in. But it was now or probably go without.

"Thank you, Blair. I'll just finish entering this information and duck home."

He wandered toward the middle of the store and she spent a minute updating the data of the last dog she'd clipped. She looked up as the customers came in.

"Mummy, they have Christmas toys for pets!"

"We sure do, Miss Tilly. Hello, Tessa," Blair said.

"Isn't this a nice shop? I didn't know you work here." Tessa Myers released her four and half-year-old daughter's hand so that Tilly could explore. "We're on a mission."

"I'll keep her out of trouble." Kaylee, almost fifteen, followed her little sister, waving at Miranda when she noticed her.

"What kind of mission?" Blair asked.

"We gave Gran a puppy. His name is Boris and he's a sausage dog. A dachshund. We thought some training treats, and maybe a nice food bowl?"

"Mummy, look!"

Tilly ran to her mother carrying a tiny mesh walking harness in a swirling pattern of psychedelic purple, orange, yellow and green. Tessa held it up with a grin.

"And I found treats to help with training," Kaylee said, catching up.

Miranda gestured to one of the stands. "There's also a matching collar and lead. Blair, the extra small sizes are perfect for the new pup."

"Feel free to browse and I'll go and find those to show you," Blair said.

Time to eat. Miranda made her way to the door to the house and glanced back. Happy customers. Happy sort-of-staff. It made for a happy day.

Much better than week-long parties.

Having those few minutes to herself to eat had given Miranda the energy for the rest of the day. The three of them had worked effortlessly together, looking out for each other and stepping in when needed. She had a lot to think about. At least at certain busy times of the year she might need a third person, perhaps someone like Blair who enjoyed the hustle and bustle of the retail side.

Except there is nobody like Blair.

Tash had gone home and the last customers of the day were heading out with Blair, who carried their little schnauzer, the final groom of the afternoon. He was so good with dogs. And customers.

And me.

Once he'd given the dog back to its owners, cheery calls of 'Merry Christmas' went back and forth. Then, as he'd done every day this week, Blair jogged to the front of the property and retrieved the A-frame which sat on the grass verge. At least with a couple of weeks to rest her ankle, she'd be back to normal duties when the salon reopened. It couldn't come fast enough.

"Why the stern expression?" Blair carried the A-frame inside.

Miranda closed and locked the door behind him. "Oh, nothing really. Just impatient with how long I've been out of action thanks to a stupid string of tinsel."

"You really haven't stopped, so no point being hard on yourself." Blair gestured to the shop. "How can you say tinsel is stupid? Look how pretty it is."

"Are you certain you want to do sport physio for the rest of your life? I mean, seeing you with customers and dogs and the shop has been quite incredible. For someone who never worked in retail before this week, you've been—'

"Bearable? Not terrible? I know . . ." he said with a grin, "unemployable."

"That is silly. I'm going to cash up and collect my dog." She started back to the counter.

"Miranda?"

The humour had left his voice. He sounded . . . hesitant.

Even as she turned to look at him, her heart began to pound. They were alone. She might see him tomorrow at the Christmas Eve party but maybe not. This very well could be goodbye until he came home for another visit.

"Kane and I are going to the parents' place for Christmas lunch."

"Oh. Um, that sounds nice."

He crossed the distance between them, stopping close enough to see there was something there in his eyes. Not hesitancy. Was he uncertain of himself? Blair?

"We'll be back in the afternoon and I wondered . . . well, I hoped maybe we could catch up. Later, I mean. As long as you're not committed elsewhere."

Little happy butterflies fluttered in her stomach.

"Yes."

"Yes, you are committed elsewhere?"

"No. That is, yes, I'd like to catch up." She finally sorted her words out.

His body seemed to relax and as he stepped a bit closer, she held her breath . . .

"Ah, good, you're still here, son."

. . . and let the breath out.

"We just closed the front door, sir."

Pop was near the counter and burst into laughter. "Sir? Are you trying to make an old man feel ancient?"

Miranda followed Blair to the counter, where he stopped to chat and she went around to start closing the tills.

"Brought down Tangles and a jug of iced tea. Would you like a glass?" Pop asked Blair.

Well, it seemed like he was only asking Blair.

"I would. Do you need a hand, Miranda?"

She held up the money bag she'd pulled out from a drawer. "Are you kidding? This is the best part of the day, counting my millions. Go ahead, I'll be along soon."

There was no argument from the men, their voices fading as she began tallying the day's takings. But when she'd done, and had turned off the computers, she paused. What had just happened? Or, more importantly, what had been about to happen when Pop wandered in?

Were you going to kiss me?

Miranda rested her hand over her heart, half expecting to feel it flip-flopping. It beat steadily.

Blair wanted to see her on Christmas Day. And he'd been nervous about saying it, so was he feeling the way she was? Was there a chance he wanted to be more than a friend? And suddenly she knew. Somehow she'd managed to fall for her best friend. Distance or not, there was no denying it any longer.

After locking the money bag into the safe, Miranda quickly freshened up, changing into fresh jeans and a blouse and releasing her hair from its ponytail. Her eyes—in the mirror—were wide and happy. How this would work, she had no idea, but just for once, she had to take a risk.

Pop and Blair were just outside and Miranda stopped to pour herself a glass of iced tea before going to join them. They were in the middle of a conversation.

"So the club renewed your contract?" Pop asked.

"They did. It makes things more secure because the drop-off rate for first year physios from clubs is huge."

"And you enjoy it?"

"Love the physio side. Helping players is incredibly rewarding, and seeing them recover from injuries and the like makes it all worthwhile."

"And Sydney?"

Miranda was frozen in place. Another year of contract . . . perhaps more. And Blair sounded happy about it.

"Sydney is amazing. Never thought I'd love a place as much as Bindarra Creek but I have to admit my life is pretty good there."

She forced herself away from the door, back into the kitchen where she leaned against the counter with her hand over her eyes.

You fool. He doesn't feel the same. He is just your best friend.

And being her best friend was good. So why were her cheeks wet with tears and why did her heart feel as if it would never beat again?

Chapter Eighteen

When Kane drove away from the house a bit after five in the morning, Blair had been awake for hours. If he'd even slept. Over and over he'd replayed the brief conversation he'd had with Miranda, trying to fathom what made her change her mind.

Asking her if she'd like to meet up with him later on Christmas Day was a big risk. She might have rejected the idea out of hand. Or accepted thinking it was still part of their friendship, because he didn't know how to say he wanted more. Not yet anyway. When she agreed, he was certain she understood. The way she'd looked at him revealed a vulnerability—a mirror of his own feelings—and if Pop Layton hadn't interrupted, the moment might well have ended with a kiss.

But even then, Miranda had been buoyant and joked about the till so why was it that only a few minutes later, when she'd joined him and Pop outside, her whole demeanour was different?

She'd sat on the furthest seat and not met his eyes as she stroked Tangles. Pop Layton had begun to ask Blair to stay for dinner and her head had shot up with a firm "No, I need an early night." There was no more banter. Her earlier spirit seemed . . . dampened. And when Pop went inside for a minute and Blair asked what time he should come by on Christmas Day, she'd mumbled something about remembering other plans.

"What happened, Miranda?"

The ceiling didn't offer any insight and he dragged himself out of bed.

Dog walking was finished for the year so there was no excuse to go to Miranda's house. Unless he went to check on her ankle. Offer to re-strap it. And he had a Christmas gift he'd gotten the other day. He had one for Pop as well and fully intended to drop it in to him after the Christmas Eve event. He even had a gift for Tangles.

He couldn't be bothered to eat. His stomach was heavy and he'd be better to get over to Lette Park and help Kane get everything ready for the crowds.

After locking up behind himself, Blair paused at the bottom of the steps. With dawn, the sky was reddish-gold and there wasn't a cloud in sight. Overnight the temperature had barely dropped and he was glad he'd thrown sunscreen and a hat into his backpack. He loved the heat out here. Sydney was too humid for his liking. Too humid and too many people. Just like he'd told Pop Layton last night.

"Sydney is amazing. Never thought I'd love a place as much as Bindarra Creek but I have to admit my life is pretty good there."

"And you plan on making a life for yourself there?" Pop had asked.

"For another year, then I'll find something closer to here."

Pop had nodded. "Better to be back home, eh?"

Blair had grinned. Pop Layton might be getting on but his eyes were keen and his instincts good. He'd worked out there was more than a friendship at stake.

"Bindarra Creek will always be home. And it's where I want to settle down and have a family."

He remembered glancing at the door, expecting Miranda to join them, but it was another ten minutes before she did.

"Oh no."

What if she'd heard part of their conversation? The part before his plans to move back.

Blair hurried to the car. Pop was helping out at the climbing rock and Miranda would arrive after work. By then, he'd have sorted out how to explain he had every intention of being back by next Christmas, and this time, for good.

"I taught you well, little brother." Kane patted Blair on the shoulder as they stood back from the climbing rock.

Soaring about eight metres high, the contraption was far more solid than Blair had expected for a mobile unit.

And far harder to climb!

But climb it he had, no less than six times to the top, clipping twenty-dollar notes where anyone lucky enough to reach the summit could collect one as a reward.

"I just have a natural talent when it comes to money. But if any are left at the end of the day I volunteer you to collect them. Legs are a bit shaky now." Blair undid the harness he'd worn. "Might need to find a shady spot to recover."

"You can recover later," Kane said. "Can you grab us some breakfast out of the esky? It might be our last chance to eat for a while. Won't be long before the party-goers arrive."

"You brought food?"

There was no answer as Kane had headed in the direction of the public conveniences, so Blair pulled the esky out from under the trestle table set up with information about the business. Inside was a container filled with sweet and savoury muffins. And a thermos of coffee was among the bottles of water and another container of sliced fruit. Was there nothing his brother hadn't thought of? He was hungry now after all the climbing.

Kane was right about eating before the party started. The morning was a blur as happy people poured into Lette Park. Families with picnic baskets found places to set up umbrellas or took advantage of spots beneath trees. Everywhere there was laughter and fun, from the giant dart board to fortune telling. As the sun beat down, Blair eyed off the dunking pool where people were having too much fun dropping different victims in the water. But he had his hands full talking about Kane's adventure tours and helping the attendants.

The climbing rock was a drawcard for kids, but lots of teens and adults were also keen to give it a go. The money at the top was even more incentive and at one point there was a decent line-up of people wanting to go up a second or third time.

Once all the races got underway—egg and spoon, sack races, three-legged races and the like—the attention moved to those events. The lull was good. Blair replenished the table with more of Kane's brochures, and bottle opener key rings they'd been handing out. The day would be worth it for the business despite being an expensive exercise. With the new awareness of the kind of adventures Kane did, there'd been a lot of enthusiastic comments.

Blair checked the time and frowned.

"Expecting someone?" Kane asked.

"I'm sure I mentioned Pop Layton offered to take some photos of the climbing rock. And you on it if you wanted some stuff for ads."

"You didn't but that was nice of him. Still have that photo he took of us playing cricket."

"Well he said he'd be along mid morning."

A group of teens headed their way.

"He's probably chatting to someone."

Kane went back to the table.

That won't help me see Miranda. Come on, Pop.

Chapter Nineteen

Today's dogs all went home with special Christmas bows or bandannas. Tash had just left after several hugs and an exchange of brightly wrapped gifts. The shop was empty for the first time since Miranda opened the door just after eight this morning and she was a bit shell-shocked as she slowly walked through the space, tidying the shelves. At least, those still holding stock. This week had been phenomenal, despite the sprained ankle.

Maybe because of it.

She'd never have gotten to know this side of Blair. The deeply caring, clever Blair who also had a knack for charming customers. Nothing was too hard for him. Nor too dirty to clean. Not even a nervous dog could stop him. The customers had adored him.

The customers weren't the only ones. Miranda leaned against one of the dogfood stands, gulping down sudden sadness.

Only a few hours ago she'd stood here facing Blair, waiting for something . . . something neither of them would have ever thought possible. And she'd let her heart lift and feel and be excited, only to crash back to reality. Of course he was going back to Sydney. It was where his life was.

"Excuse me . . . are you still open?" The voice was quiet. A woman stood just inside the doorway, as if unsure she was welcome.

"Please, do come in. Not closed quite yet."

"I was sure I'd be too late. I'm after a Christmas present for my . . . for someone's dog. Would you have anything suitable? A toy perhaps?"

"Of course. Come over here and let's see what's left after a very busy morning. For an adult, or puppy?"

"Banjo's about six months old. Mix of kelpie and border collie."

"Beautiful. Well, these are really popular, and tough, so they hold up against sharp teeth." Miranda picked up a thick, rubber stick-shaped toy. "They bounce, so are great for throwing, and have a small squeak to encourage play."

"Oh, that's perfect!" A small smile formed on the customer's lips and she nodded. "I'll have that, thank you."

It took no time to ring up the sale and walk the customer to the door with a cheery 'Merry Christmas'.

Door locked, Miranda released a long sigh.

She'd made it. Goodness knows how many people had been in the shop in the past week. Looking at the stats was something for another day but she was confident the shop's bank balance was a whole lot healthier than before.

Despite her heartache, she was proud of herself and, mostly, of Tash and Blair. Without them, who knows what might have happened? Cancelling grooming clients most likely to reduce the workload which was no way for a budding business to have its first Christmas trade. She turned off all the lights and cashed up the tills, humming something festive. It was time to begin winding down. Enjoy the festivities at the Christmas Eve party and then spend time with Pop.

"I hoped maybe we could catch up. Later I mean. As long as you're not committed elsewhere."

Blair's words echoed in her head.

There'd been a few minutes last night when her heart had sung and she'd begun planning an evening with him and Pop and music and sitting outside with lots of leftovers and presents. Nothing too intense. Not yet. No need for them to be alone when the day was all about family.

So why had she told him there was another commitment? There was nothing stopping her from spending part of Christmas Day with him. Blair was her best friend and she'd seen the confusion, then hurt, in his eyes. But deep down she knew why. The longer she spent with him, the harder she fell.

And he was leaving soon. Her heart couldn't bear to lose someone else.

Her parents were long gone.

Nan was gone.

Better to put her walls back up.

Losing Blair was not an option; being friends was enough.

Lette Park was a hive of activity. Miranda parked as close as possible to avoid walking too far. She'd passed Pop's car a bit further along. He'd said he'd bring a picnic blanket and chairs for them both. Despite the long week and working this morning, her ankle was holding up pretty well and she moved more freely once she reached the lush, soft grass.

What a wonderful event this was! Bore water was used to keep the grass so inviting, and with the shade trees it was a picture here. All around were different fun stalls and barbeques, and the grass was dotted with picnic blankets.

But everyone's attention was on the fantastic new splash pool. She'd arrived during the official opening and stopped for a moment to listen to the speech by the mayor, Barry Donaldson. His lovely wife, Gloria, was at his side, and Miranda made a mental note to catch up with them a bit later to say hello.

Is the whole of Bindarra Creek here?

As the ceremony ended to loud applause, music began in the rotunda.

Miranda gazed around. Pop was somewhere. He'd probably have set up the chairs then gone to help Kane and Blair. Or at least take some photographs. While most of the world moved to taking images on their smartphones, he still swore by his camera and various lenses.

She went in the general direction of the climbing rock, a huge construction which stood out in the park. On her way she was stopped by a couple of customers wishing her Merry Christmas and praising her about the shop. How lovely to hear people say they'd be back in the new year. The climbing rock was busy, with a couple of attendants helping Kane work with people. Blair was behind a table, chatting to someone with a brochure in his hands.

But Pop wasn't around.

Miranda stopped walking, leaning her weight on her good foot while she scanned the area. There were plenty of folk she knew and a lot of fun-looking activities, but he wasn't in sight.

She rang his phone. It went to his voicemail and she left a message that she was at the park now. Her eyes moved back to Blair and he glanced up, his face breaking into a broad smile.

Those silly emotions started up again and she was torn. She could smile back and tell him she'd made a mistake last night, or walk away and pretend she'd not seen him.

It didn't matter because he was heading her way and

she had no chance of staying ahead of him. She pushed a smile onto her face as he stopped a couple of feet away. He wore shorts and a t-shirt, the latter of which was a bit sweaty and clung to him in all the right places. Dragging her eyes from his chest, she blushed at the humour on his face. She'd not meant him to notice her scrutiny. It was embarrassing.

"Where's Pop?" she blurted.

"Around somewhere. How was the shop? I could have been there if—"

"The shop was fine. So Pop was here?"

Being so close to Blair was horrible. Wonderful. Awful.

"Miranda, he's most likely trading stories with some of the RSL guys. Why are you worrying?"

Because he disappears and when he does, it frightens me.

"You're right. I'll go check over there."

She'd only taken a few steps when he caught up.

"I don't need help finding him." Her words were delivered in a flat tone. It was the only way not to be cross about . . . well, everything.

"Can we talk? I need to clear something up with you."

What? That you want to remind me you're going back to Sydney?

Had he hoped to have some kind of short term fling? Come home every so often and have Miranda hanging around as his friend-with-benefits?

"Of all the nerve!" Miranda stopped dead, hands on hips.

Blair hadn't expected her to stop and had to turn back. He clearly had no idea what was wrong, from the look of confusion on his face. "Of all what nerve?"

"Expecting me to . . ."

Even as the words came out she realised how ridiculous they sounded. Blair wasn't that kind of person. He tilted his head, waiting for her to finish her sentence.

"I have to find Pop."

With that, she strode away.

Actually, she hobbled quickly. But he didn't follow and when she reached the RSL tent she glanced back. He hadn't moved, apart from crossing his arms. For a moment the urge to go back and explain her feelings and worries almost won, but it would be for nothing. Lifting her head, she went in search of her grandfather.

Thirty minutes later she had nothing other than a painful ankle and growing frustration. She'd phoned again and sent messages to Pop with no response. Asked at every stand. Stopped people who'd know him. She'd found his picnic blanket and chairs with an esky. Inside was water and oddly, a small, wrapped gift with no card.

Miranda gazed around, her eyes misting up as worry tumbled around her stomach. She might have to go home and make sure he wasn't there, unwell or . . . something.

Her heart thudded and her stomach churned.

You need some help. Go and ask.

Over at the climbing rock, Blair was helping a young woman into a harness. She was giggling. Flirting. The heat of the day had got to Miranda. All she wanted was to tell the woman that Blair was taken. How silly was she being?

A young couple walked by, hand in hand, eyes on each other. Their love was a living thing. Well, good for them. She'd decided long ago that love was for other people. People who had time to spend with each other. To start a life together. A family. It wasn't for her.

Focus on Pop.

He was missing. If it was anything like the last few times, he'd be fine, but today was hot and it didn't look as if he'd taken any water from the esky.

By the time she returned to the climbing rock, Blair

was free again. Drinking from a bottle of water. When he saw her, he put the lid back on the bottle and waited. He wasn't giving anything away so maybe he'd finally had enough of being pushed away.

She gulped. This wasn't something she could do alone.

"Blair? Would you help me find Pop?"

Chapter Twenty

Blair had known Miranda long enough to back off when she spoke a certain way or cast a particular look at him. They'd rarely argued over the years of friendship but there were times he pushed the boundaries a bit with his sense of humour, or tried too hard to get her out of her comfort zone. Today he didn't want to back off. She was upset about more than Pop Layton being hard to find.

This is about us.

She'd virtually snapped his head off and that was *after* she'd checked out his chest and turned bright red. The sooner they were able to have a proper conversation, without distractions, the better.

He felt her eyes on him and looked up. No grandfather in tow. And panic etched in her face.

"Blair? Would you help me find Pop?"

There was a waver in her voice.

"Of course. Hang on a sec."

He dashed around the climbing rock to where Kane was spotting a climber.

"Sorry to interrupt. Miranda can't locate her grandfather and I need to—"

"Go. We're good here."

On his way back Blair grabbed an unopened bottle of water.

"Drink." He shoved it into Miranda's hands. "At least you've got a hat on."

"Excuse me? I'm not ten."

"No, you're not. I apologise. But please have some water while I try Pop's number, just in case there was a network issue or something."

She scowled but opened the lid while he dialled. Voicemail.

"He may have left the phone at home. Or in the car. Whereabouts have you looked so far?"

Miranda rushed her words, pointing as she spoke. He wanted to hug her and tell her it would be alright, but was smart enough to keep his hands to himself.

"You've covered a lot of ground. And people will tell him you're looking for him so it's just a matter of time. Are you up to walking back to where he set up the picnic?"

In a couple of minutes they were at the spot and Miranda sank onto one of the chairs. "I just need a moment." She rubbed her ankle.

"Once we find Pop, I'll grab my kit and give your joint a bit more support."

"This isn't about me, Blair. I'm fine. But where on earth is he?" She looked around. "He definitely said he was going to take photos for Kane and I expected him to go to the opening of the splash pool to take more." Her eyes turned back with an intense gaze with something behind it. Fear? "You are one hundred percent sure you haven't seen him at all today?"

"I haven't. But, Miranda, we've been so busy at the climbing rock that he might have swung by. Maybe he took photos while Kane or I were on the other side and then went to catch up with a friend."

"What friend? I've asked everybody he knows."

She stopped rubbing her ankle and sipped some water.

"Idea. Let me do a quick run around and ask again. You stay here in case he returns."

"I can't, Blair!" Her eyes glistened. "This isn't the first time recently that he's done this. Saying he'll be one place then wander off. I'm really worried that he has dementia or something, not that I know anything about it. But he's all I have in the world. Him and Tangles. And if anything happens to him . . ."

The tear trickling down her cheek was too much for Blair.

Before he could stop himself he'd dropped to his knees and wrapped his arms around her. She leaned against him and he thought he heard, "I can't lose you too." It couldn't be that. She must mean Pop, but having her in his arms was perfect even if the situation was the opposite. He needed to find Pop Layton and then tell Miranda how he felt and what he planned. See if she was willing to wait a little longer for him.

The moment ended as she straightened. He kept hold of a hand and she let him, her eyes searching his face.

I love you so much.

Now wasn't the time to tell her. Or perhaps it was.

"If you can do that—run around to look—there's one place I've not gone so I'll head there," she said.

"I'll only be a few minutes if you want to wait for me."

With a shake of her head she gently pulled her hand from his and stood. "Two people in two places are better. The day is so warm I worry he'll forget to drink water. I'll take one for him from the esky."

"Where are you heading?" Blair got to his feet.

"The oak trees in the far corner. He used to come down here to photograph them, lying on his back to get the branches and leaves in the different light. Over that way." She gestured. "It'll take me a few minutes."

"Okay. I'll meet you there."

Rather than watch her painfully limp away, he took off in the opposite direction at a sprint. He only had one place to go and needed to get there fast.

The person in charge of announcements carefully wrote down Blair's words and promised that Mayor Donaldson would be back within a few minutes.

That done, Blair ran to the climbing rock. With the upcoming arrival of Santa, the rock was quieter again and Kane leaned against it with a bottle of water.

"Can you call me if you see Pop Layton? Miranda is beside herself."

"Do you want me to come and search?"

Blair had never loved his brother as much as he did this moment.

"Thank you. Not at this point. Once the event finishes, if we haven't located him, then yes. Until then, do your thing."

"My "thing" is running itself. The offer stands."

For some reason that he had no idea about, Blair threw his arms around Kane. "Appreciate that, mate." Just as quickly, he released him and took off toward the oak trees.

Despite the heat of the day and his multiple climbs, running was easy on the thick grass. And he had a destination. If Pop Layton was at the oak trees then Miranda could relax and enjoy the remainder of the day.

And if not?

It didn't bear thinking about.

He'd almost caught up with Miranda by the time she went around the largest of the oaks, a mighty tree with a truck thick enough to hide several people from his view. He slowed to a walk, drawing in deep breaths, and ran a hand over his forehead.

She stopped in her tracks and both hands flew up to cover her mouth. He couldn't see what she was looking at but it was downwards, towards the opposite base of the tree. Blair wanted to call out, to ask what was wrong but no words would come.

Was it Pop Layton?

Chapter Twenty-One

I can't walk much further.

Pain in her ankle, frustration with herself, and worry about Pop mingled with the rush of emotions from being close to Blair. His hug had only been from sympathy, she knew that, but it messed with her resolve to keep him at arm's length. Tears weren't her thing, but lately she'd been in them at the drop of a hat.

Once she found Pop she'd go home. Drink a lot of water, sit with Tangles—who was chilling in the cool of the house—and read a book.

In the distance, children's laughter, as they played in the new splash pool, tempted her to stop there on the way and put her sore legs into the water for a while. First she'd insist Pop come home as well and not let him out of her sight until after Christmas Day.

He was nowhere to be seen. Hopefully Blair had better luck because there was no reason for Pop to be lurking behind a tree. She'd checked each one as she'd hobbled down and there was only the one left—the beautiful old oak.

"Pop?"

No response or movement. Another waste of time. But she'd come this far, so might as well check the other side.

Her heart almost stopped as a shoe—Pop's shoe, for sure—poked out as she rounded the trunk. Another two steps and she halted, unable to move other than cover her mouth so she didn't scream.

Pop was leaning against the trunk, his eyes closed.

You can't be . . . You can't leave me . . .

But his chest was rising and falling and, bit by bit, other details cut through the panic.

An open book with its pages facing down on his outstretched legs.

His hat placed on the ground.

A second set of legs beside him.

Her eyes travelled up those legs to the face of a woman.

Miranda took several steps back as Blair reached her, his mouth open to speak. She moved her fingers into a 'shh' motion and moved even further away. He followed, his eyes widening as he saw the couple.

"I think they're asleep," she whispered. "Do you know her?"

Blair took another look and shook his head.

Pop was here, hidden away from the party, with a strange woman. The woman had to be close to Pop's age and had a sweet face with short white hair. There was a small picnic basket nearby with two empty champagne glasses resting against it.

"No wonder they were over here if they wanted a quiet drink." Blair spoke softly, close to her ear. "I might need to drive his car back, heh?"

"What on earth, though? I mean . . . who is she?"

The vision of chocolate cake in Pop's fridge popped into her head.

"Someone special. See their hands?" Blair asked.

How did I miss that?

Their fingers were entwined.

Unsure if she was relieved to find Pop in no worse state than sleeping off a glass of champagne on a hot day, or shocked that he had been seeing someone and kept it secret, Miranda shook her head. She shoved all the thoughts and feelings down to unpack later. When she was alone again.

The PA system crackled.

Blair took her hand. "Should we let them be?"

Mayor Donaldson's voice boomed across the park. "Attention, everyone. If Carter Layton hears this, would you make your way to the climbing rock please? Might need a climb myself. Carter Layton, time to climb."

Pop's eyelids opened and his head turned to the woman beside him. "Wake up, dear. I think Miranda's looking for me."

The woman's eyes fluttered open and then widened as she noticed Miranda and Blair, who'd not had time to retreat.

Pop followed her line of sight and grinned. "Whoops. Didn't mean for us to take a nap." He started to get up and Blair crossed the distance to give him a hand. The woman was on her feet before Pop and went straight to Miranda with a tentative smile.

"Hello, Miranda. I'm Beryl. And it was me who suggested we sit down here to share the picnic and the mini bottle of bubbles. I'm so sorry if you were looking for Carter."

Miranda shook the other woman's outstretched hand in a daze. What was she supposed to say? Was Pop serious about Beryl? It looked like it.

Which meant he must be over Nan.

How does that even happen? How could he not love Nan anymore?

"Er, nice to meet you. I have to get going. I have . . . something. I forgot to turn off the lights in the shop."

Head down, she hobbled away, not caring if she seemed rude. She didn't know how Pop would get home but it was where she had to go. Right now.

"Miranda! Don't hurry off, child." Pop huffed a bit as he caught up. "Stop a minute, please."

"I think Beryl is very nice, Pop. I do need to—"

He put his hand on her arm and she sighed as she stopped. There was no way he could make her look at him and he had better not say anything about Nan because then she'd make a fool of herself.

"Kiddo . . . I gave you a scare. Time just got away from me and—"

"I phoned you. Blair phoned you. And I left messages."

"Phone's at home. Noticed when I got here. I got a few pics of the climbing rock while they were busy, so I guess they didn't see me. And then when Beryl arrived . . ."

"Go back and enjoy your day, Pop. I'm really tired and sore."

He leaned down and kissed her forehead. "Go on then. We'll talk later."

The sound of Santa coming in on the fire truck filled the grounds as she stumbled away, heart heavy. First her ankle. Then Blair. Now Pop and Beryl.

Christmas was ruined.

A long, cool shower followed by an hour sitting with her feet up and a glass of iced tea helped, at least a bit. Tangles seemed to know Miranda was upset and he followed her around the house, then lay beside her, checking every so often that she was okay.

Pop's car went up the driveway just after four and, a few minutes later, Blair jogged past on his way out, not even glancing at her house.

"You embarrassed everyone, Miranda." She hadn't meant to.

Walking away like that at the park was rude. But staying might have led to words she had no right saying aloud. How she felt about Nan and Pop was not for public airing; nor were her feelings about Beryl . . . or any other woman taking Nan's place.

Too rattled to relax and read, Miranda opened the door to the shop, Tangles dropping onto the concrete floor and lying on his side. It was cooler in here, and if she kept the lights off this wasn't a bad place to spend a while. She might as well remove the decorations.

The Christmas tree was first. All the baubles went into their own box, as did the tree. Next year she'd source a real tree in a pot that could be planted on the property, but time had gotten away this season. Then she worked her way around the store with a trolley and boxes, removing oversized bows and baubles, low-lying tinsel, a foot-high Santa from a shelf, and some coloured lights.

That chocolate cake in the fridge that day—it had to have been from Beryl. And the day Pop got back really late from shopping and said he'd caught up with a friend? Beryl.

Miranda stopped pushing the trolley as her stomach churned. All the time she'd thought he was losing his faculties, disappearing with no feasible explanation, he was probably with Beryl. Where had he even met her, and how long had this been going on?

She almost laughed aloud at herself.

You sound like a parent, not a grandchild.

He had every right to happiness and it wasn't her place to judge.

Being alone on Christmas Eve was making her grumpy. She parked the trolley with its boxes in the small storeroom and picked up a long pole she kept behind the door. There was a hook at one end which made it ideal for her next job. And then she'd make her way up to Pop's and put things right with him.

Behind the counter she lifted the pole and hooked the end of a strand of tinsel. With a tug, it came free. Then, she twisted its other end around the hook and freed it. Scooping it off the floor she glared at it. "If it wasn't for you and your friends I wouldn't be in this mess. And I don't mean the ankle!"

The tinsel didn't care and she piled it onto the counter.

Most of the ceiling display was a flower-like arrangement with tinsel ends together in the middle of the shop going out to the walls in gentle loops. She worked her way around the outside, dropping the ends one by one until the centre of the shop was like a waterfall of green and red glittering strands.

"Very pretty," a voice remarked. A *man's voice*.

Miranda jumped, dropping the pole, which hit the concrete with a clatter. "There is a door, Blair. You have a hand which is perfect for knocking."

He raised his hands and gazed at them. "Two, actually. May I offer them to assist?"

She scooped up the pole and moved closer to the strands. "Thank you for taking Pop home."

Blair leaned down to scratch Tangles behind the ears. The dog hadn't bothered to do more than lift his head but was quite happy to be petted, his tail thumping. "He feels terrible about upsetting you."

"Upsetting me? Because he left his phone at home and was nowhere to be found?" Now she sounded like the parent again. "All this time, I didn't know . . . that those times he wasn't where I expected . . . he was with someone." Miranda stuck the hook into the middle of the tinsel, trying to catch as many strands as possible. "And it's his business anyway."

"We need to talk. You and me. About us." Blair straightened.

"Sure. This is where you remind me about your new life." She tugged gently. Nothing happened. "You don't need to, Blair. I'm fine with it."

"You are?"

How had he got so close? She barely had space to lift the pole again. But she did, and began tapping the ceiling panel to lift it enough for the tinsel to loosen.

"That's disappointing. You being fine with it. Because I'm not," Blair said.

"Don't worry about me. I'm not interested in you or anything . . . Sorry, what did you say?" She lowered the pole and rested it against a stand, her eyes on his face. He couldn't mean what she thought.

What I want.

His eyes were alight and when he smiled it was just for her and made her heart skip a beat. "I love my job. No doubt about it. But it isn't because of where it is. It's because I help people and am pretty good at what I do." He touched her face. "I think I've fallen for my best friend and if she feels the same, then we have a problem."

"A problem?"

"My contract runs another footie season."

"And then you'll renew it."

He shook his head slowly. "Not if my best friend can wait for me to move back."

A shiver of delight gave Miranda goosebumps. "What will you do for a job?"

One strand of red tinsel fell onto Blair's head; Miranda

reached up to remove it and suddenly she was in his arms and their lips were mere inches apart. If her heart raced any faster she'd faint and end up back on the floor where he'd picked her up from only days ago.

"I'd like to kiss you now," Blair said.

"I think you should."

His arms tightened around her and he lowered his head.

In a riot of colour, the rest of the tinsel flower slipped from its twist tie and tumbled onto them both. Tangles jumped up and barked as they tried to free themselves of the mixed up strands, both laughing as they made things worse.

Well and truly caught up in the tinsel, Miranda whispered, "this is better than mistletoe."

"A million times better," Blair's voice softened.

The laughter trailed away as they gazed into each other's eyes.

Tangles woofed again.

"I think he's telling you to hurry up." If Blair didn't kiss her right this minute . . .

"Anything to keep the dog happy."

Blair touched her lips with his. A gentle brush. Tentative. And then he drew Miranda so close against his body that she could feel the thudding of his heart. Or was it her heart? Sparks of electricity flew through Miranda as they kissed until all the breath left her lungs.

And when Blair raised his head, his eyes were glistening. "Miranda, look at us."

"If anyone comes in they'll think we are ridiculous. Dressed up like a tree."

He grinned and kissed her again.

Tangles lay down with a grunt.

"We were always meant to be and if you were in any

doubt, then take this tangle of tinsel as a sign. I love you, Miranda Layton."

Her heart was going to burst with happiness as she raised herself up on her good foot.

"I love you, Blair. Even if you are red and green."

Wrapped up in sparkling strands, Blair kissed Miranda.

Epilogue

"It took me a long time—years—to even begin to think about what Nan said I should. And now that I have, I understand why she made me promise to open my heart again, when I was ready." Pop touched a framed photograph of his wedding day. Nan and he were sharing a kiss while their friends and families clapped and confetti fell around them.

His hands shook a little as he lowered them and Miranda covered them with her own and leaned her head on his shoulder.

"Before she died, we had a long talk. About you mostly, and our wonderful, incredible life together. And she looked me in the eyes and told me there'd be a time when I'd find love again. I said it was impossible because I'd already had a lifetime of love, and she smiled and reminded me nothing is impossible. The first time I met Beryl—who was helping some poor soul who'd fallen on the footpath—I remembered our conversation and knew that somewhere, your nan was smiling down on me."

"I'm so sorry about how I reacted," Miranda said. "And I am so happy that you are happy."

Pop gave her a long look. "And I have to apologise for not letting you know what was happening and why I occasionally disappeared. But I had no idea you thought I was losing my marbles."

"I wouldn't put it like that!"

Tangles trotted down the hallway from the direction of the kitchen, stopping halfway with an expectant expression and wag of his tail.

"You've been fed, dude," Miranda said. "And I'm quite certain Blair has been sneaking you some extras in the kitchen."

"Did I hear my name?"

Blair's head appeared around the doorway and Miranda's heart skipped a beat at his smile. This was so new. And so wonderful.

"Does this mean dinner is served?" Pop asked with a grin.

When Miranda told Pop that she'd invited Blair over, he'd insisted on moving their planned Christmas lunch to a dinner. And she had to admit, spending the afternoon with Pop prepping and cooking was a joy. When Blair arrived an hour or so ago, the two men told Miranda to get off her feet, and who was she to argue? With no guilt whatsoever, she'd taken a book and gone out onto the front verandah where an overhead fan kept the temperature bearable. Occasionally, hearing laughter from inside, she'd raise her head and smile. How quickly things had changed for the better. Then she'd settle back again and delve into the mystery story.

After a bit, Pop had wandered out and suggested they make their way inside. It was then that he'd stopped at the photographs and talked about his growing 'affection', as he called it, for Beryl.

"Ready as it ever will be." Blair disappeared.

"Why didn't you invite her to our dinner?" Miranda asked Pop. "It wasn't because I was upset, was it?"

"Not at all. She has four grown children in Tamworth and went there this morning to spend a couple of days. And besides, this is our time, kiddo."

"But you're sharing it with Blair."

Pop shrugged. "He's always been part of the family. Now come and see what we did while you were reading."

How could anything possibly top the day? Blair's Christmas was as perfect as it could be.

Mid morning, he and Kane had driven over to their parents' house—part of a retirement village with benefits, such as a golf course for Dad and book club for Mum. Their home was a single level house big enough for them and the cats, with a small but pretty garden. The gifts went down a treat and even the cats were keen to try out the new post with its multiple levels and snuggly bed at the top.

Lunch was different from those growing up. A new tradition, according to Mum. It began with a walk around the village, delivering a tiny basket of homemade goodies to each and every resident. Blair had eyed off the treats and Mum noticed, pressing a basket each into his and Kane's hands before they left after lunch. That was the other big difference. In the past they'd have had a big, cooked lunch followed by Mum's delectable pavlova. This time it was lots of salads and seafood. Dad mentioned they were trying to look after themselves a bit more these days.

Blair's heart had dropped for a while as the reality sank in that these wonderful people were aging. But they were so happy with their new life that he'd left feeling content. Kane had felt the same. Their parents meant the world to them and today it felt like they were in a good place.

Arriving at the Layton property he'd been greeted with enthusiasm by Tangles, then Pop had given him a hug, and finally, when Pop wasn't looking, Miranda had given him a quick kiss on his lips before taking his hand and leading him to the kitchen. The hour or so helping Pop was good, filled with talk of their common loves, such as cricket.

"That's how Tangles got his name, wasn't it?" he'd asked.

"Yup. Loved Max "Tangles" Walker from the first time I saw him play cricket, with that peculiar bowling action of his. And when we brought home a twelve-week-old pup whose legs were at odds with each other, he just had to have the same name. Tangles it is."

He stood back from the kitchen table with a smile. While Miranda had enjoyed a well-deserved chance to put her feet up and read, he and Pop had gone to *town* decorating in here. Red tablecloth and napkins. White plates on green placemats. Red and green Christmas crackers. A sumptuous spread with turkey, roast vegetables, several salads, and homemade bread rolls.

"Here we are, son," Pop said.

And then Miranda was at the doorway, her mouth open and eyes wide as they swept over the table and then to his face. "Wow. This looks beautiful."

You are beautiful.

"Come on, you two. Not getting any younger here and I've waited all day for this." Pop collected a bottle of sparkling wine from the fridge. "Seeing as I've talked Blair into sleeping in the spare room tonight, I think we should enjoy this."

"You do quite like your champagne now, don't you, Pop?" Miranda teased.

"Nothing wrong with a few bubbles."

Blair pulled out a chair. "For you."

Miranda sat with a warm smile and soft 'thank you'.

127

Tangles planted himself next to Pop with a steely gaze.

"Um . . . what have you done to my dog?" Miranda began to laugh. "Poor Tangles."

Wrapped around his neck was a loop of red and green tinsel. He clearly didn't care at all; his sole focus was on persuading Pop he needed to share Christmas dinner.

Before sitting beside Miranda, Blair removed the tinsel. "You're right. I can think of somewhere else it belongs." He unwound the glittering strands and draped some around Miranda's shoulders as he sat. "New tradition. Whoever is tangled in tinsel has to kiss."

Pop's eyes shone.

Miranda leaned closer. "Are we tangled?"

"I think we are."

She wrapped the other ends of the tinsel around him and touched her lips to his. "Merry Christmas."

More in this series...

Thank you for reading my Bindarra Creek Christmas Romance, Tangled by Tinsel.

Welcome to the heart-warming joy of nine sweet, Christmas romances set in a small rural town. Experience happy-ever-afters along with the up-lifting good cheer of love and life in Bindarra Creek, and meet again our community of interesting and charming people. Each story can be read as a stand-a-lone and can be read in any order.

The Mistletoe Wish by Suzanne Gilchrist
A Clever Christmas by Annie Seaton
Mistletoe Magic by Erin Moira O'Hara
Christmas Jinx by Susanne Bellamy
Tangled by Tinsel by Phillipa Nefri Clark
The Grinch of Bindarra Creek by Lindsay Douglas
Mistletoe and Blue Jeans by Linda Charles
Christmas at Forrest Glen by Rhonda Forrest
A Cowboy for Christmas by Lauren K McKellar

Visit **https://bindarracreekromance.com/ bindarra-creek-christmas-romances/**

Our Bindarra Creek Christmas Romances are the fifth series set in our fictional small town.

The fourth, is the Bindarra Creek Mystery Romances – a series of seven exciting and suspense-filled romances which again can be read alone.

About the Author

Phillipa lives just outside a beautiful town in country Victoria, Australia. She also lives in the many worlds of her imagination and stockpiles stories beside her laptop.

She writes from the heart about love, dreams, secrets, discovery, the sea, the world as she knows it… or wishes it could be. She loves happy endings, heart-pounding suspense, and characters who stay with you long after the final page.

With a passion for music, the ocean, animals, nature, reading, and writing, she is often found in the vegetable garden pondering a new story.

www.phillipaclark.com

By Phillipa Nefri Clark

Rivers End Mystery Romances

The Stationmaster's Cottage

Jasmine Sea

The Secrets of Palmerston House

The Christmas Key

Taming the Wind

Martha

Daphne Jones Mysteries

Daph on the Beach (prequel)

Till Daph Do Us Part

The Shadow of Daph

Tales of Life and Daph

Bindarra Creek Rural Fiction

A Perfect Danger

Tangled by Tinsel

Maple Gardens Matchmakers

The Heart Match

The Christmas Match

Doctor Grok's Peculiar Shop Short Story Collection

Last Known Contact

(A gripping standalone crime/romantic suspense)

Simple Words for Troubled Times

(Short non-fiction happiness and comfort book)

Prefer Audiobooks?

The Stationmaster's Cottage

Jasmine Sea

The Secrets of Palmerston House

Last Known Contact

Simple Words for Troubled Times

Till Daph Do Us Part